Love's Crossroads

A Novel

By

L.M. Lapham

Paperback ISBN: 979-8-9885953-0-4

Hardcover ISBN: 979-8-9885953-1-1

L. M. Lapham

This literary work is a product of the author's creative imagination. The names, characters, and events depicted therein are entirely fictitious. Any resemblance to actual persons, living or dead, or real-life events or locales, is purely coincidental. The primary objective of this narrative is to explore the artistic potential within the realm of fiction and captivate readers with an imaginative story.

L. M. Lapham

Dedication

To the first man who taught me about love.

"My DAD"

I miss you!

L. M. Lapham

Acknowledgment

May love always be in your heart along with a song. Keep loving wholeheartedly, and never stop believing that you can have it all.

To all those who have inspired me along the way and taught me what really matters in life.

Love, Laughter, and Living a Great Life.

Thank You.

To my amazing family who have always believed in my dreams.

Thank You.

To my handsome son, you will always be my greatest gift. And to my loving husband, YOU are my rock!

I Love You! 

About the Author

L. M. Lapham has traveled around the world, spending extended time in Paris, London, and New York. She lives in Austin with her husband and two dogs.

Love's Crossroads is the premiere novel of the series that will take you to the world of love and romance.

Contents

Chapter One

The springtime on the East Coast was a magical season, where blossoms adorned every branch, and the air carried a scent of new beginnings. This was true on the college campus of Princeton University, one of the eight Ivy League schools in the country. On the prestigious Princeton campus, Brian, a freshman hailing from the vibrant streets of New York City and pursuing International Business, eagerly awaited the upcoming Spring Break. As his last class of the day, American Literature, drew to a close, his professor set forth an intriguing project and asked his students to research and interview the most extraordinary person they had ever known. This could be either family or friend.

After thinking about it for a moment, the first family member that came to Brian's mind was his paternal grandmother, Kathrine. She had lived the most spectacular life all over the world, experiencing the glitz of catwalks in Paris and the allure of the big screen. As the bell rang, signaling the end of his class, Brian's mind was already set on the subject of his project. The Professor had specifically asked the students to bring their projects to life. Brian felt confident enough to work on this project, and his grandmother's life story could be a home run. He wanted to delve into the life story of his grandmother and rushed out of the class to make his way back to the dorm room.

Brian knew that to truly grasp the essence of his grandmother's life, he needed to visit her in Miami and hear stories from her. Reflecting back on his life as a young boy, Brian could still remember his father telling him in detail how beautiful his mother's life was to him. While traveling all over the world before his father was born, she enjoyed her life in every capacity. She had been a single parent, raising Brian's father with unwavering dedication while instilling in him the values and morals she learned from her own upbringing. Her most treasured accomplishment was raising her son alone.

Also, having three brothers had kept her in shape with all her affairs, ultimately advancing her confidence with the men she met. While growing up, the small town in Texas they called home seemed way too small on most days. In the quaint surroundings of a small town, she dreamt of exploring the world, meeting people from all walks of life, and embracing the enlightenment that came with worldly experiences. She knew that life would call her to become enlightened on every level around the world. The many extravagant experiences in her life would prepare her to evolve into a spiritual being.

When asked about her greatest accomplishments, without hesitation, her answer would be raising her son to greatness with her book of life experiences.

Overwhelmed with excitement, Brian called his grandma Kathrine to share his plans. "Grandma, it's Brian, your grandson." He paused to wait for her response. "I'm coming to Miami for Spring Break and would love to visit you if that would be okay with you?"

She answered, "I would love to see my favorite grandson. What time is your flight? I will have Henry pick you up."

Brian wasn't really sure exactly who Henry was but agreed to the invitation without hesitation. "My flight will be arriving Sunday night around 5 o'clock."

The excitement in her voice encouraged him to respond with, "Looking forward to being with you, Grandma."

They both ended the call with love for each other.

Brian knew that this experience was going to be a positive one, not only for his project in class but for himself, too. He was silent for a moment, thinking that the life story of his grandmother would be one he could treasure forever. Glimpsing love through his grandmother's eyes, he was entranced by its enchanting magic. Filled with inspiration, he eagerly looked forward to meeting her soon and couldn't wait to write her extraordinary story.

He organized the second part of his spring break trip with his friends. He planned on meeting them on Thursday in South Beach, adding a touch of adventure to the journey ahead. Spring Break for college students was a time to party and relax after months of hectic routine. However, this trip meant more to Brian than just a party; it meant spending quality time learning about his heritage from his grandmother. The flight arrived at Miami International Airport, and just like grandma Kathrine promised, Henry stood waiting for him at the baggage claim. He held a sign that read, "Welcome to Miami, Brian."

Filled with emotions, Brian walked up to Henry to proclaim his arrival. "Hello, Henry. I am Brian. I hope you haven't been waiting for very long?"

Henry politely shook his head and replied, "Don't you worry about that. All that matters is you're here, and I'll make sure to safely take you to your grandmother's home. She's eagerly anticipating your arrival."

As they walked over to baggage claim to retrieve his bags, Brian wondered how long Henry had known his grandmother.

"How did you and my grandmother meet?" Brian inquired.

Henry looked over at Brian and answered, "I have known your grandmother for more than 30 years. She volunteered at the local Nursing Home where my mother lived for five years. In a world where we are often disconnected from each other, your grandmother became very close to her and took care of her needs up until her last breath. I have never forgotten your grandmother's dedication to comforting my mother in her last years of life." He paused and took a deep breath as if lost in the memory. Clearing his throat, he began again. "After she passed, I felt lost and confused for many months. But your precious grandmother took me in as one of her own family members, and I have been taking care of her ever since."

Brian's heart swelled with pride for his grandmother, eager to express his deep appreciation for the joy she had brought to so many lives.

The atmosphere in the car was filled with awe and expectation as they departed from the airport. Brian couldn't wait to wrap his arms around his grandmother, showering her with gratitude for the boundless love and compassion she had selflessly shared throughout her life. Brian knew that this reunion with his grandmother would liberate his emotions, connect him to his heritage and fulfill a commitment to understanding how it all came to be for him.

As the car turned into the driveway, nervousness overwhelmed his body. The front door's lights cast a beautiful silhouette of his grandmother, standing with a radiant smile on her face. Brian jumped out of the car and ran up to her to hug her neck. "Grandma Kathrine, it's so wonderful to see you."

"It's about time my only grandson has come home to see me," Grandma Kathrine said, embracing him with overflowing gratitude. "I am so happy that you have made the trip to visit me. Throughout all my travels in life, the moment that has always excited me the most was arriving to greet my love. The love you have for others is of utmost importance, Brian," she said warmly, and Brian nodded in agreement.

"I have waited my whole life to finally hear about your beautiful adventures. As a young boy, I fantasized about living a life like yours because of the stories my father shared with me."

"I hope those stories were filled with happiness and somewhat the truth," she added.

They both started laughing together.

"I know; why don't you tell me your story just the way it happened?"

She smiled at Brian with a playful wink. "You got it."

Henry interrupted, "I have taken your bags up to your room that your grandmother has arranged for your stay."

"Thank you, Henry," said Brian.

A petite woman emerged from the kitchen and asked, "Anyone hungry?"

Brian was more than delighted to take her up on that offer. "I am starving and would love to have something to eat."

"Welcome, Brian. I'm Maria, and I will help you feel right at home because this is your home. This home is everyone's home. This is your grandmother's belief when it comes to opening up her home. So, please follow me into the kitchen, where I can get you something to eat."

While Maria prepared a dish for him, Brian settled into a chair at the table, his gaze wandering around the room. The walls were adorned with pictures of his grandmother alongside public figures and Heads of State, a testament to a life dedicated to traveling the world. The enticing aroma from Maria's cooking and memories on the walls suggested the layers of living a life full of stories. "Grandma, I would love to hear all about your life story," Brian expressed his eagerness to delve into the remarkable journey of his beloved grandmother.

A moment of silence embraced the room before she spoke, "I would be honored to indulge in my fantastic experiences that produced a lifetime of memories. Most of all, the memory of the choices I made along the way, offering unconditional love and support."

Grandma Kathrine began unfolding the beginning of her beautiful life story in segments, and her grandson eagerly hung on to every word, brimming with sheer excitement.

As she began sharing her story, the room came alive with the essence of her experiences. Taking a deep breath, a twinkle in her eye, she started narrating the chapters of her life.

Chapter Two

The month of June started off to be exciting and eventful, commencing with the celebration of my birthday, a festivity that extended throughout the entire month. Over the past year, I had been dating an Englishman from London, leading to countless trips back and forth between our two cities. As he arrived to spend the weekend with me, he expressed the desire to make it a committed relationship. Little did I know that this weekend would mark the turning point in our journey together. That weekend made me realize that this would not be the lifestyle I would choose for myself. After spending the weekend in New York together, I decided to tell him we would remain friends. But was that easy to do? My thoughts threatened to engulf me. I wondered if I was making the right choice or if I would regret it later. Nevertheless, I knew I had to make a decision. And I had to make it soon.

It was a difficult decision because of all the exciting times shared with friends and family; however, my heart made the decision for me. Deep within, my heart spoke with unwavering clarity, guiding me toward a choice I knew I must make.

As I stood there, watching him drive off to the airport, a profound certainty settled in my heart - this would be the final goodbye. Emotions swirled within both of us, leaving us vulnerable. He called me to say "Goodbye" from the car with a potent sadness in his voice. He already knew the answer but still asked, "Is it over between us?"

"I need some time to figure out what I want for my life," I responded, taking a moment to gather my thoughts.

When one door closes, another door opens, and it opens wide.

The next week was spent sorting out the feelings of a love that turned out to be a stepping stone to the life I was about to embark on. Amidst the cheerful calls from friends and family, it was Chelsea, my best friend, who had the uncanny ability to uplift my spirits and bring comfort during those days.

The night of June 14th marked the beginning of a new chapter in my life. The evening began as a simple dinner outing at a local Asian restaurant in the neighborhood.

We could laugh about nothing and everything at

the same time. This was exactly what I needed after the breakup with my London lover. "Let's step out and try a new Karaoke Irish bar," Chelsea suggested with a big smile on her face. We both laughed at the same time and agreed this was what our souls needed. After settling the bill, we set off to the Irish pub, Fleming, to sing and drink. On this summer evening, it was a big night in New York City for hockey.

The New York Rangers were playing at home in the last game to decide who would win the Stanley Cup. Just as we entered the place, the winning celebration of the New York Rangers began.

Upon entering the establishment, the distinct scent of spilled beer overwhelmed my senses. The place was bustling with passionate Ranger fans, all gathered to celebrate the team's victory. As I made my way to the bar, my eyes quickly scanned the crowded space, and there he was – a striking, American-Italian-looking guy wearing patchwork shorts and a vibrant, eye-catching shirt. Our eyes locked from across the room, and an unspoken connection seemed to form instantly. The bar was packed with people celebrating the New York Rangers win of the Stanley Cup, and the energy was electrifying, to say the least.

Even the regular patrons at the bar could sense that this was a special moment. We proceeded up the stairs to find a table where we could enjoy the view. As we looked on, I couldn't help myself from watching the guy with the patchwork shorts on. Soon enough, he made his way up the stairs, stepping closer to me. The first words out of his mouth were, "What are you girls doing in a place like this?"

I answered back with a smile, "Will you turn around?" Without hesitation, he turned, showing off his backside.

He then asked me, "Why?"

I replied, "Damn, you're as cute as a BUTTON." This was the beginning of our conversation.

I asked him if he would like to join us for a drink and a song. "I'll buy the drinks if you two would sing the songs," he said with a charming smile. I knew as soon as he opened his mouth that he was from Boston. The accent was so strong and profound that you couldn't help but pick up on where he was from. His handsome movie star appearance was utterly irresistible, and an undeniable attraction sparked between us from that very moment. As the night progressed, our connection grew stronger with each round of drinks we ordered. He generously bought rounds of drinks and shots for everyone around us. It began to get crazy.

After a few attempts at karaoke with Chelsea, we both decided to sit back and enjoy watching others take the stage. We liked the idea but had little confidence to follow through. As the night progressed and the crowd gradually thinned out, Chelsea decided it was time to drink up and leave before she reached her limit. I, on the other hand, had just gotten started. We sat at the bar until closing time and decided to make a move. As the night wound down, Buttons asked me if I would like to accompany him. "I have three sisters, and I am a very nice guy. You can trust me," he assured me.

I responded playfully, "Well, I have three brothers, and if you try anything funny, I'll have to kick your ass."

We both laughed and decided to leave Flemings.

We were the last ones in the bar at this point, so onwards and upwards we had to go. Neither one of us had a plan on where to go, and being too intoxicated, I didn't think to ask. We got into his car, which was parked along the street just in front of the bar, and away we went to his place. Having lived in New York City for several years, I thought we would just drive over to his apartment down the street. I had not asked him where he lived and found myself leaving Manhattan. I never thought of having him drive us to my place, which was just down the street.

We drove to a small town outside of New York City, and without a doubt, I knew nothing of this area. Once arriving at his place, we went inside his two-story house, which he shared with four roommates. He had told me more information than I could remember, but I heard it again the next day. Once inside the house, you could tell that five single guys lived there and liked to think of themselves as still somewhat in college.

"Do you want something to drink, like water or a beer?"

I replied, "I will just take some water."

There was an innocence about him that charmed me to no end, mixed with a little sadness. I liked him. We made our way up to his room and walked inside, which needed a whole lot of help. It had aluminum foil around the light bulb, and some home projects came to mind. I didn't want to ask, but I looked around and thought to myself, "What have I done now?" This seemed very careless on my part, but being a bit depressed after the break-up with James, I stepped out and thought, "What the hell?" Some experience waking up the next day and finding yourself in a foreign place. Foreign in the sense that nothing looked familiar.

Buttons mentioned that he had a very important meeting to attend at work. Our minds were cloudy, but the physical attraction was there for both of us. We kissed all night until the sunrise lit up the room. The morning arrived way too early, and getting up seemed impossible. I felt very uncomfortable at that moment and thought of how the hell I would get home. "If you wouldn't mind waiting in my car until my meeting is over, I will drive you back to your place in the city and take you out for lunch."

I thought about it for a moment and agreed to his proposal. I knew that this would be the easiest way home. I had time while sitting in his car to realize something about myself. This realization I had about myself was clear that love comes without telling you, just through the heart in its own time. I had decided to open my heart and allow love in at that moment in time, and it felt amazing. This was the beginning of a love story that would have so many peaks and valleys. But at that moment, all I could think of was my bed. After lunch, he dropped me off at my apartment. I went to sleep for the entire day.

The next day felt like an eternity, and I found myself a bit confused regarding my emotions toward Buttons. While I was certain of our strong connection, thoughts of uncertainty crept into my mind with phrases like, "Who knows if we shall meet again?"

He appeared to be a nice guy, but perhaps it was just my hangover messing with me. Around 6 p.m., he reached out to check on how I was feeling after last night.

I wasn't sure how to act toward him when I answered the phone. "Hello, Buttons."

He laughed, then replied, "How are you feeling today?"

I quickly answered, "Feeling so much better today, and thank you for a great time last night." We both laughed about the events that had happened to us.

"That was some night, right?"

Without hesitation, I replied, "That was one hell of a night."

He answered, "When can we get together again? I will be in the city all week, so you name the night?"

Excitement surged through me as I eagerly replied, "Any night would work for me this week. Let's try for Thursday."

So, there it was. Thursday night would be the next time we would meet up again. I really felt excited about having plans with him. Through the next couple of days, anticipation began to build up for my date with Buttons. What I remembered most about Buttons was his great smile and sexy eyes. Whenever I looked into his eyes, I knew that there was something truly special about him.

The way we kissed made me want more moments spent with him. He was a gorgeous guy with an athletic build and an exceptional kisser. We had so much passion for each other from the start that I knew it would only get better with each encounter.

The night arrived for us to meet up. I had it all working for me with the sexiest dress I could find in my closet. I spent two hours at my favorite hair salon, having my hair styled and getting a fresh manicure and pedicure. He called to ask for directions to my apartment. "Where is your place in the city?"

My response to his question was, "I'm on 71st, why?"

"Will you meet me in Midtown because I've just finished a meeting close to a great Italian restaurant on 54th?"

"Sure, no problem." I agreed, looking forward to the evening ahead.

Well, this was not the way to impress me by any means, but he was not your conventional kind of guy. I knew there would be some adjustments to how I liked to be treated. Picking me up on the first real date was one of them. Due to the situation, I decided to bend the rules a bit. After all, what are rules for, if not to be bent? I arrived in front of the restaurant and paid the cab bill. I approached the front door and looked inside the bar. There he was, standing at the bar, waiting for me with flowers in hand. The feelings rushed through me once again when I saw him.

Feelings of love and passion engulfed my entire body. I knew, even on our first date, that there was something undeniably special about this relationship, though I couldn't quite pinpoint it just yet. I was certain that time would unveil the magic of it all. I gave him a warm hug and greeted him with, "Hello, handsome. Have you been waiting long?"

He replied, "No, I just got here." His accent was so strong that it made me laugh just to hear it again.

We had an incredibly enjoyable encounter with each other. His physical appearance exuded strength, with muscular arms, a great body, and a captivating smile that could set you free. As he began to tell me about his family in Boston, I found his background quite colorful and intriguing. Growing up in the suburbs of Boston with his parents and three sisters, his family faced challenges like any other typical American family. The passion between us intensified over dinner, and all I could think about was the desire to kiss him in private. Thoughts of making love to him grew stronger with every gesture he made toward me. After our dinner, he suggested, "Let's go dancing somewhere."

He proposed a nightclub that played music from the 80s, which just so happened to be the music we both grew up listening to in school. As we danced together, it felt like the beginning of our physical attraction toward each other. We moved in harmony to the beat, and I couldn't help but feel the strong connection between us. We danced until 1 a.m. to music that transported me back to my sweet sixteenth year of life. I allowed myself to relish the freedom of that time and enjoyed the night with Buttons, drinking shots of whatever we could create and dancing to our heart's content.

We swiftly hopped into a cab, returning to my apartment. Once at the front door, I eagerly stepped out of the cab but found myself staggering as I approached the entrance to my building while he took care of paying the cab driver. "Are you going to make it, beautiful?" I heard Button's voice from a distance.

In a slightly slurred manner, I mumbled, "You better believe I am."

With a determined spirit, we passed the doormen and made our way to the elevators. As the elevator doors opened, we exchanged a passionate kiss, stepping inside without pressing the button for my floor. An unusual feeling washed over me. Being a bit inebriated, my first thought was that we might be stuck. But then, it hit me—we had simply forgotten to press the button for my floor.

Buttons made a remark, "Should I push the floor, or do you want to stay here all night?"

My first thought was to call him a smartass, but with my motor skills not operating at full capacity, I decided to simply push the number 5, and up we went. Opening the door to my apartment went fairly easily, and walking through the door was even easier. My two poodles were there to greet us, jumping up on Buttons and barking at us, which eventually turned into affection. He seemed indifferent towards them, but he pretended to like them.

***

As Brian sat at the dining table, he listened intently to my captivating tale of love and adventure. "What an introduction and spontaneous decision to go home with him!" Brian knew this must have been exciting to experience, but the uncertainty of who this man was kept it a mystery. Maria looked over at Brian to check on him while he enjoyed the meal she had prepared for him. "Do you need anything, Brian?"

"I am perfect, Maria, thank you." The story meant so much coming from his grandmother herself.

"Brian, I hope that I am not sharing too much for one evening. I am feeling tired and will have to stop for the night. Maria will show you to your room after you have decided to retire for the evening. Please make yourself at home. I am so thrilled that you're here with me for the week," Grandma Kathrine said, her voice and eyes radiating love and warmth.

"Goodnight, Grandma."

"The best is yet to come tomorrow, and let's have some fun exploring the story of two lovers," she added with a playful tone.

Everyone laughed together, realizing that she was absolutely right.

Chapter Three

As morning awakened the house, a beautiful sunrise enveloped the surroundings, filling everyone's soul with a sense of serenity. All gathered in the kitchen, drawn by the inviting aroma of freshly brewed coffee. "Good morning, Brian," Maria greeted him softly.

"Good morning, everyone," Brian replied. His enthusiasm was almost too much to handle. Grandma Kathrine and Henry were seated around the table, each with a cup of coffee in hand.

"How did you sleep last night, Brian?" Grandma Kathrine inquired.

"Like a baby," Brian smiled, expressing his gratitude for the warm hospitality.

"We like hearing that, sweetheart. Would you like some coffee?" Maria offered.

"Yes, please."

Maria handed him a coffee cup and guided him to the cream and sugar on the counter. "Make yourself at home, Brian," she said warmly.

"I will indeed," Brian replied.

"Would you like some breakfast, Brian?"

Brian needed to have his coffee first before eating

a full meal. "I would like to wake up with this hot cup of coffee, then I would be up for some breakfast," he replied with a smile.

"Now, Brian, explain to me what is required from me to help you complete your project," Grandma Kathrine said as Brian sipped his coffee.

"Just express to me, in your own words, what life was like for you, from the opportunities and choices you made along the way."

"Well, then, let's begin."

She recalled the moments in her life that would shape her future. After reflecting on a full life, she began to tell Brian more of her story.

*****

I'll start with an American girl on holiday in the South of France who meets her Prince Charming. A discovery that would change my life forever. The story began when I accepted an invitation from a good friend to join them and others in their Villa in St. Tropez. The timing was perfect. After the breakup with my English lover and meeting Buttons last month, I wasn't really sure where my next step would take me, so this invitation came at the perfect moment. When planning to stay for a week, there was plenty of organizing that needed to be done. I arranged for my two poodles to stay with Carol, their second mother. I prepared everything and headed out to the airport with my favorite driver.

Lucky had been driving me for years, and this time, we had a lot to talk about before boarding my flight to St. Tropez.

"Where are you off to this time?" asked Lucky.

"Oh, you know, some fancy spot along the French Riviera," I replied.

He just laughed and smiled back at me from his rear-view mirror. We pulled up to JFK Airport just in time.

"Thank you, Lucky, for the company and laughter before I leave for Europe."

"You have a safe trip, Kathrine," he said with a smile and a wink.

"Thank you. I am off to meet my Prince Charming."

After my arrival, I planned to hire a car service from Nice to St. Tropez, where I would meet up with my dear friend Ashley, whom I had met in Aspen while skiing on New Year's Eve. She arrived a day before I did and already had plans organized for the week. The couple who had rented the villa were friends of hers from Aspen.

They had it booked for the whole month of July. Once on the grounds, I could see why they were staying for a month.

The view was breathtakingly beautiful. All the photos I had seen didn't come close to capturing its true beauty and charm. The entire interior was wonderfully furnished, exuding a timeless charm that I immediately fell in love with. As for my room, I was pleased to see that it was a cozy place for getting ready and sleeping. My first hours in the villa were spent relaxing by the pool and unwinding from my flight from New York.

Everyone had been out the night before and spent this time recovering from it. They had met a group of people from Belgium and arranged for lunch by the beach for today.

I asked Ashley, "What are these new friends like?"

She replied, "You will really like this one guy who is with them."

Now, she had my attention.

"He is a Baron from Belgium."

I chuckled and thought to myself, now, this is the right way to start off my holiday in St. Tropez. I decided to start getting ready for lunch. Ashley had told me when

I arrived to be ready for lunch at 1 p.m. I needed a little extra time to look my best due to the long journey from New York. I dressed up with just a little extra something to look gorgeous. Everyone at the house piled into one car, and off we went. The beach was a good half an hour from where we were staying up in the hills.

Once we arrived, Jake, who had rented the villa, dropped off all the girls and then went to park. We entered the restaurant and found a table by the beach with our new friends from Belgium. My first impression of the new friends was that they all seemed happy to receive us for lunch. Ashley introduced me to everyone, saying, "This is my good friend whom I spoke of yesterday."

She turned to her right side, grabbed the Baron's hand and reached for mine, and said, "I think you two will find that you are a lot alike. Baron, this is my good friend Kathrine."

After this introduction, I felt speechless. "Hello, everyone. I am so happy to finally be here with you."

Then I looked at the Baron and asked if I could sit next to him. His delightful smile invited me to sit without words. He was a very tall, distinguished-looking older gentleman with a very happy-go-lucky way about him. I could recognize this through his eyes. I knew at that moment that life, as I once knew it, would never be the same.

The weather was perfect for a day at the beach, and the energy at the table between everyone seemed electrifying. After my first glass of wine, I knew that this would be a hell of a day. Lunch at the beach in St. Tropez was bound to be the most interesting lunch ever. French music, fresh seafood, good wine, and plenty of great conversation. Laughter and love entangled the conversation with intrigue for hours.

The Baron turned to me and asked, "Would you like to walk along the beach with me?"

I answered, "I would love to walk with you."

We had so much to talk about that it seemed like we were old friends. The walk we shared together ignited the magic for us.

As Grandma Kathrine introduced the Baron to Brian, she detected a sense of perpetual love that he was forming between the characters in her story.

He asked her, "At this point, did you know that you were beginning to have feelings for the Baron?"

"I knew the minute we met that I could fall in love with him. He seemed to be a very kind man and extremely knowledgeable in many areas, such as both current and past events. This enlightened me on every level."

Grandma Kathrine's motivation to share every detail with Brian was to help him get an outline for his school project. She could tell his interest in working with her extended to a clear understanding of what really went on in her life. She wondered what Brian might be thinking about as she continued to tell her story. He was a very mature young man with a curious mind. He needed to know exactly how and why it happened, and he reminded her of his father at that age.

She continued on with her story. "Where was I again?"

"Summer in St. Tropez.," he answered back promptly.

"Oh, yes, back to my story."

***

After we left the beach, we drove back to the villa in the hills. The first thing we all wanted was another drink, a cigarette, and the pool. The music playing on the speakers by the pool was a song that reminded me of Buttons: 'Mr. Jones.' By The Counting Crows. Just hearing the song made me smile, and I missed him without a doubt at that moment. I felt strong affection for him, but I wasn't sure why at that moment. So, I deflected my thoughts and focused on enjoying the beautiful surroundings of the South of France. Time was precious in that place, and I had to prepare for the evening ahead.

The plan was to go for dinner in town and then meet up with our friends from Belgium. We went to a cozy restaurant in the harbor, a place where everyone seemed to know everyone. As soon as we arrived, I knew that I would enjoy the atmosphere surrounding us. Everyone spoke French, including myself, a skill I developed after living in Paris for three years while working on modeling assignments.

We left feeling no pain and singing songs off-key due to the alcohol intake we all had in our bodies. The next stop was the piano bar in town, where we would meet our new friends. Once inside, I knew the evening would be fulfilled.

The Baron immediately jumped up to greet us at the door. "Good evening, my American friends."

With a warm welcome like that, I knew we had arrived.

I answered, "Hello, my Prince Charming. How are you tonight?"

I tried to impress him with my French, but I think that goal was already accomplished.

First things first. He ordered us all champagne and then asked who wanted to sing first.

The piano player wanted someone to sing with him, and that loving feeling engulfed me. Up to the piano I went, ready to sing whatever the Baron wanted to hear. Singing happens to be one of my favorite things to do in life. Feeling confident, I was open to singing anything. And then, I heard the words "New York, New York." As the piano began playing the piece, a strong rush of feelings came over me about the city and Buttons. I wondered where he might be and what he could be up to. But I quickly blocked any emotions to truly enjoy the moment.

After singing the song, I headed back to my seat. The Baron clapped and stood up as I approached him. "Bravo, Darling!" This was the beginning of a romance that could only happen once in a girl's life. I kept telling myself to embrace it, enjoy it, and live every moment of it. So that is exactly what I did. I lived it in every aspect. A professional photographer came over to us and asked us to pose. It was time for a photo. She snapped many photos of us, including photos of everyone sitting with us, and then smiled at the Baron to buy all of them. More champagne, more cigarettes, and great conversation consumed us for hours.

When it was time to leave, the Baron turned to me and spoke softly, "Would you like to go with me for a midnight swim at my place?"

"Yes, I would love to."

My friends looked at me like I was crazy, but they knew it was my decision. Just at that moment, I felt a profound sense of freedom that I had lost for some time.

We left the piano bar holding hands and with a kick in our step. I believe both of us were extremely excited to be with each other. As we traveled to his hotel, we passed many beautiful sites of nightlife in St. Tropez. There were many beautiful people out in cafes, walking from place to place with a carefree attitude. The café had a sophisticated and comfortable ambiance, ideal for having a cup of coffee under the warm lighting and elegant décor. This was so inviting for me to experience. As we drove along the edges of St. Tropez, a certain magical feeling came over me —excitement for the moment in front of me.

Chapter Four

As we arrived at the Baron's beautiful hotel, my only thought was that this was meant to be in my life, so embrace it! We walked outside through the lobby area and out to a massive, manicured sanctuary. The grounds left me speechless, with such appreciation for their beauty and charm. We made our way up to his room and entered his bungalow through an archway covered with amazing Ivy. Once inside, we started kissing passionately, holding each other tightly.

Our souls were joining together and dancing with each other. This was a very magical time for both of us. Even though we had just met, we connected on many levels. I turned to him and asked him if he was still up for that swim. With a slight hesitation, he responded, "If it's all right with you, darling, let's have a morning swim." I had no problem having a swim in the morning.

We embraced each other with our lips and began kissing one another passionately. This extreme affection for each other led to making love all night. I felt so connected to him that nothing held me back. The lovemaking continued for several hours until we fell asleep in each other's arms in a warm embrace. We gazed into each other's eyes, our hearts beating in perfect unison. The morning arrived with a luminous sunrise that awakened both of us to a certain feeling of being in paradise.

"Good morning, darling."

These were the first words I heard as I opened my eyes, and without skipping a beat, I answered, "Bonjour, Moi Cheri."

We both looked at each other with calmness. It's funny how people can automatically find peaceful thoughts for another human being without even knowing them.

If only the world could share this viewpoint. I reached over and began kissing the Baron all over his body. I wanted more of him, and before long, we began to make love to each other again; this time, more intense feelings came over me. This was not just sex with a stranger, but this was making love to my soulmate. Later, we were off for a morning swim to celebrate the beginning of a beautiful relationship.

The grounds were so spacious, with exotic flowers and scented fragrances that seemed to fill the pathway with a heavenly feeling. A feeling that makes you want to get up and dance at 8 a.m. The sequence of events placed us around the pool for breakfast. In the South of France, this would consist of coffee, croissants, fresh fruit, and a cigarette. Breakfast of Champions, at best, seems to help with a champagne hangover. The weather seemed perfect for a morning swim, so into the pool I went, with only my bottoms on. This excited the Baron very much, as well as the rest of the guests, who had just awakened to find the party still going on in the pool. The pool was exactly what I needed to begin the day. Time just stood still while I sat in that magnificent pool with so much beauty surrounding me. After enjoying our petit déjeuner, I knew it was time to return to my friend's place, but I didn't want this moment to end. I got out of the pool, and we walked up to the room to change into my clothes. The ride home was enjoyable for both of us. We planned to spend our day together, learning more about each other. I gathered my things at the house and spoke to Ashley for a brief moment. She seemed unhappy with my decision to leave with the Baron, but I knew that it was my decision to live my life. I told her, "Let's meet up for dinner later."

She answered back, "Sounds good, just call me later."

***

At this point, Grandma Kathrine stopped and asked her Grandson, "Sweetheart, let's go for lunch. I know this charming little French Bistro along the beach." He looked excited to venture off for the moment. She could feel in his heart that maybe this story was beginning to shed some light on her as a person. She really wanted him to get her full story, and as sexy as it might be, she believed that he could handle it from a spiritual and emotional viewpoint. Much like his father, he was a mature young man with a kind, gentle soul carrying wisdom from life's journey before his time.

She asked him, "How do you find the story up to this point?"

His response surprised her: "Grandma, I never knew all of this about you. The lifestyle you must have been living back then must have been exciting. The choices you had to make to find your way took courage and compassion toward others. How did you handle all of of?"

She took a deep breath and replied, "I made sacrifices and gave more *of* myself than I gave *to* myself." At that moment, she saw an expression on his face and knew that he really understood what she meant.

"I cannot wait to hear the rest of the story, and I hope this isn't too painful for you, Grandma."

She quickly answered, "This is a story worth telling, and I am enjoying this time with you."

He smiled with a big grin and kissed her cheek. She felt so blessed at that moment to be in his company.

They drove along the beach to a charming Bistro, and so many memories flooded Grandma Kathrine's mind. She wanted to start with her love story again and asked her grandson, "Would you mind if I started telling you more of my story while we are driving?"

He spoke without hesitation, "Not at all, Grandma."

'I'll start back by spending the afternoon with my new friend."

***

I couldn't wait to experience this new feeling with my new lover. He was so interested in so many areas. He had extraordinary knowledge of Art and owned the largest collection of Gustave Courbet, a French artist. He was extremely knowledgeable about fine European wines. He adored the finest things in life and loved spoiling the women around him. We could talk about anything and everything. He told me that his passion for the United States was based on a sequence of events that had happened in his lifetime, and I felt a real desire for him to visit the United States. Off to lunch, we proceeded. He knew this great restaurant along the harbor in St. Tropez. The theme for lunch was seafood and good wine. I began to see that he enjoyed drinking fine wines as much as I did, another common trait we shared.

Our conversation continued to entertain us both. The combination of good wine and stimulating conversation had me enjoying the lunch with much pleasure. He asked me, "Would you like to visit me in Belgium, so I can introduce you to my world?"

"Most certainly," I answered directly, with no hesitation. The feelings between us became stronger with every awakening moment. After finishing lunch, we strolled along the narrow streets of St. Tropez to shop for a new gift. He wanted to purchase a piece of jewelry for me that would remind me of our first real moment together. He ended up buying me several items from the boutiques. Clothing, several new pairs of shoes, jewelry, and whatever he felt like purchasing. I enjoyed the attention he gave me and allowed him to lavish me with gifts. It had been some time since I had received this kind of attention, and I wanted to enjoy the experience. He mentioned to me that we were going to dinner at this beautiful French Chateau.

We went back to his room and prepared for the evening. He ran the bath for us to enjoy together. Being alone with him felt so natural, as if I had known him all my life. I loved his hands caressing my body as he washed my back. He worked his way around to the front of my breasts and began massaging them. By this point, he had asked for my hand and taken me to the bed, where he made love to me as passionately as the previous night. I didn't want to stop feeling him, even though I knew we had dinner plans. But the intensity of our intimacy was so strong that it made us indulge in each other more and more. "You are the best lover that I've ever had, my darling. I want to kiss every inch of your body every time I look at you."

I smiled and got up from the bed to go into the bathroom to shower. He followed me and grabbed my neck with his hand around my back to kiss me. "I want to make love to you all day and night. We will continue this after our dinner."

As we began to dress for dinner, he presented me with a beautiful necklace that he had bought in town. "This is a token of my love and appreciation for meeting you and looking forward to our love affair together." I could hardly stand still for him to attach it to my neck. I felt so much love for him at that moment. It was a beautiful diamond heart necklace.

"What a beautiful gift. I'm truly overwhelmed with your kindness," I said, as he hugged me and spoke French in my ear. "Oh, la la."

I blushed and kissed him on the lips. "Shall we go, darling?"

"Yes," I answered.

We arrived in the lobby, and his driver signaled to him that he was ready. We took off along the Cote d'Azur, the French Riviera, for dinner, with his driver taking care of us. He knew himself well enough to hire a driver for our convenience. The drive was so beautiful along the Cote d'Azur that it was beyond words. Once we arrived at the restaurant, a team opened our doors and escorted us into this magnificent Chateau. It felt like an episode from The Lifestyles of the Rich and Famous. We were then greeted by several people who showed us our own table outside in a bungalow environment. I took in the place and realized that the elements had aligned just perfectly for us this evening. The full moon lit up the villa and bestowed us with luminous magic from above. There was a very large, solid black Great Dane dog looking at us from the front of the restaurant.

You couldn't miss his stern focus on the crowd of people. A beautiful French chandelier hung above our table, along with lights that were strung from side to side across the space. To put it simply, I was mesmerized. The Baron kissed my hand and began to read from the menu to me. "First on the menu is a glass from the bottle of their own champagne."

"Sounds perfect," I thought to myself. Then he asked the waiter to bring us a bottle of their finest champagne. After the waiter poured the champagne into a crystal flute, the Baron stood up and stared at me, saying, "A toast to the woman of my dreams."

The Baron proclaimed his love for me at that moment. I felt overwhelmed with excitement for everything that was happening to me. One day, I'm flying on a plane from JFK; the next day, I'm celebrating life with the Baron. I knew at that moment that this would completely change my life forever. How would I handle the lifestyle? Would it be the fairy tale that comes once in a girl's life, if at all?

I embraced it with a toast to the Baron, "To my Prince Charming. May this be the beginning of something very special."

I knew that everything I had experienced up to

this point in my life had prepared me for this moment and beyond. He began to kiss me at the table, and I responded with a passionate kiss. The dinner was about to be served, and I didn't even feel like eating.

The Baron had organized everything before our arrival, so they had prepared a fixed menu with everything already ordered.

The first course was caviar and foie gras, which seemed appropriate, being that we were in France. We fed the caviar to each other and kissed between each bite. "Darling, how do you like this place?"

Speechless was the first word that came to mind.

"Je t'adore Moi, Cheri." Which meant I adored this place. The second course arrived, and it was a beautiful fresh fish prepared with lemon and olive oil.

It came with a side order of green beans and a potato pancake on the side plate. A salad arrived after the meal to clean the pallet for dessert. Many sips of champagne later, we arrived at the beautiful Crème Brûlée being delivered to our table. This was a French favorite among the locals and worldwide. It's a custard with sugar sprinkled on top of it and placed under a broiler until it forms a perfect brown top layer of sugar. At that point in the evening, I just wanted to kiss him and feel those good feelings for him. I asked him if we could skip the Crème Brûlée and go back to his place for dessert. His response delighted me: "I'll have them wrap up the dessert and ask them to have the car ready to leave just as soon as we finish our champagne."

Feeling frisky from all the touching and kissing we displayed for each other at dinner, it was natural to begin again in the car.

The driver enjoyed our playful spirit with each other without resistance. I asked him, "How was your evening?" but in French.

"Super, merci beaucoup." He replied.

I could only think about getting back to the room for a private love session. Our feelings for one another had intensified with all the champagne we had been drinking. Behind closed doors, the freedom to express our love for each other was ours to explore.

There was a tender moment in all the physical attraction where I knew I wanted to spend quality time with him. Speaking without words, only through the eyes, became the language between us. After the lovemaking, we were off to the pool for a midnight swim. The water felt so comforting, almost like soaking in a pool filled with love. I asked with sheer pleasure, "How are you feeling?"

Words could not capture the expression on his face. "I am so happy, my love. I want to spend the week with you; would that be ok with you?"

Without hesitation, I replied, "I would love to spend the week with you." At this point, those words began the inseparable journey that would cross over all boundaries. The next couple of days were spent shopping, sunbathing, laughing, loving, and making memories. I felt like a Princess each day with the Baron and never wanted these feelings to ever end. Those were the best days of my life. Every adventure with him was a first for me. Introducing me to another world made of beauty and precious moments.

Meanwhile, my friend Ashley was extremely happy for us, without the malice that some girls might have felt towards another's happiness. We organized a night together to enjoy the performance of a famous jazz musician who invited us to his home in St. Tropez. I had known him for several years from my winters spent in Aspen. His international popularity had spread across the globe, and he was one of the most prominent contemporary instrumental jazz players in the world. His home overlooked the harbor, which was jam-packed with Yachts. It was a beautiful St. Tropez evening filled with live music and fine wine while listening to jazz on a beautiful July evening. The music could be heard all through the town, and love was in the air. The feeling of love among friends could be felt very strongly that evening. If only the world could have been a part of that evening. I thought to myself that World Peace might have a chance if everyone could feel the music. The night was a moment that stood still in time for everyone. After the music stopped, we drove back to the Baron's Hotel, where we had one last glass of champagne together at the bar. The connection between the two of us continued to grow stronger, day by day and into the night. As we enjoyed our time together, the week flew by. I knew that I would be flying back to New York tomorrow, and my thoughts were that I might not see the Baron again.

I became overwhelmed with emotions and reached out for his hand. "Darling, you know that our life together has just begun, and without a doubt, I know this is true love," I said.

He replied, "Sweetheart, I want to come to New York in two weeks and spend a beautiful holiday with you in your hometown."

Filled with joy and emotions, tears started to flow down my cheeks. I was overjoyed, knowing we would be together in two weeks. The thought of having another moment in time with this lovely person excited me endlessly.

The next day arrived earlier than expected, and I prepared to meet Ashley at the Helipad, where we would take a helicopter to Nice from St. Tropez to catch our flight back to JFK.

Chapter Five

As Grandma Kathrine and Brian arrived back at her home along the beach, she felt so much passion from within her soul. She knew her grandson could feel the love in her heart for this man as well. Looking over at him, she embraced the emotions from reflecting back on her life. Remembering the abundance of love overwhelmed her. She asked her grandson, "Would you like to have dinner on the terrace with me around 7?"

He replied, "Of course, I would be honored to accompany you for dinner."

Grandma Kathrine smiled and thought, what a fine young man he is towards women. She asked Maria to prepare dinner for two and have it ready to be served by 6:45 p.m. Maria was thrilled to see her so engaged with her grandson.

Being served dinner alongside her grandson on the terrace overlooking the Atlantic Ocean was a serene experience.

Brian looked at his grandmother so sweetly. "I would love to hear some more of your story, Grandma, if you feel like it."

"Avec plaisir, Moi Cheri." He grinned with delight at her love of the French language.

*****

As my memory has it, the flight wasn't as long going home as it was going there, and knowing that I actually gained my full day back had me feeling at ease. My dogs had been staying with Carol, who watched them better than the kennel for me. However, she charged me the same amount, but it was worth it; Pierre and Pascal really loved Carol and her family. In a hurry, I dropped off my bags at the apartment and rushed over to pick up my kids, Pierre and Pascal. I couldn't wait to see them and tell Carol all about the beautiful story of my holiday spent in St. Tropez.

The dogs kept jumping up on me, wanting some attention from me. "Hello, Moi petit Chien." They had been to Paris with me several times and loved it when I spoke French to them, or so I thought in my mind. I had brought gifts back for Carol and her family, so I watched as they opened them with much appreciation. After spending time with them, I had to head home for a nap. I felt a bit jet-lagged and decided to rest for a while. Awakened by the phone ringing, I jumped up to answer it, and with much surprise, I heard Button's voice on the other end.

"Hey, are you back?" he asked with excitement. I could feel his anticipation of meeting up with me. "I am back from a fabulous holiday in St. Tropez," I replied with equal enthusiasm. "I'll tell you all about it when we get together. When will you be in the city?" I hoped he would suggest meeting tonight. "We could meet for a drink tonight after my meeting downtown," he said, wanting to see me as much as I wanted to see him. "Where would you like to meet?" I asked. He suggested that he would pick me up, and we could decide together. "That sounds like a plan. See you around 7:30 p.m.," I said, feeling excited. I needed everything worked on, such as a manicure, pedicure, eyebrow wax, bikini wax, and a workout. The workout was first on the list of things to "get ready."

After finishing everything on my list, I felt exhausted from it all, so I decided to take a thirty-minute nap. Preparing for a fun-filled evening, I found the perfect dress to wear for the evening.

The doormen buzzed me up and informed me that I had a male visitor. I thought that it was a bit early for Buttons; I couldn't imagine who it was downstairs. It was a delivery from the Baron. The little blue box gave away that it was purchased at a certain store. I giggled all the way back to my apartment. The card read, "To my darling, I hope you had a nice trip home, and I will see you in two weeks. Love you." As soon as I opened the box with anticipation and excitement, the earrings jumped out at me with their brilliant shine. A pair of diamond and sapphire earrings. All I could do was scream with excitement. My heart began to beat just a bit faster with gratitude for this man. He knew how to make me feel like a real woman, or at least like a princess. After admiring my new gift thoroughly, I went back to getting dressed for the evening. Adding the final touches to everything, I put the new earrings on. The doormen rang me up again, but this time they announced, "Buttons is here for you." I answered, "Tell him that I will be right down." I gathered my things and proceeded to take the elevator downstairs.

When the doors opened to the lobby, I heard, "Hello, beautiful." I looked around for the voice in the lobby. "Hey, you!" I gave him a hug and then a kiss to express my feeling of joy to be in his arms again. The connection between us became real at that moment. I had thoughts of skipping dinner and making love back upstairs, where we could just order food to be delivered.

Those were my only thoughts, and because we had yet to have sex, I reminded myself to behave. "I am ready, handsome. Did you miss me?"

He replied quickly while he looked into my eyes. "I am so glad that you are back." Without a doubt, I knew that we were falling in love with each other. "Let's go for dinner." He said and took my hand while walking forward to greet the doormen. "We will be back later." Both men stood there just smiling with a grin on their faces for us.

***

Now, the story really started to take shape, with both love interests going in two different directions. Brian could feel his grandmother's sensitive energy at this moment. He asked her in a very quiet voice, "You loved them both very much, Grandma. That's my feeling, so what happens next?"

She thought to herself, "What a wonderful life I was about to embark on with two fabulous men, both from totally different worlds, but the differences impacted my life without a doubt for the better."

The full moon's positive energy filled her thoughts of the past as she felt she had shared enough for one day. "I'm beginning to feel a bit tired now, so we will pick back up tomorrow morning."

"I understand, Grandma. I enjoyed listening to your amazing stories of a beautiful life. I feel privileged just to have this time with you," Brian replied.

"I'm thrilled to share this emotional yet beautiful story with you. After all, this is how you came to be as well."

Both of them could feel their love for each other at that moment.

"I'll see you in the morning. Please help yourself to anything you might want from the kitchen. I am off to bed. Goodnight, sweetheart."

With that being said, she went to her room.

The sunrise inspired Grandma Kathrine to wake up and take a long walk along the beach, contemplating feelings from yesterday that felt like today. She began to imagine that youthful woman from years ago with so much life ahead of her and no real direction to hold her back. There are no boundaries, and borders to hold the heart back from experiencing love on all levels. As she headed back from her walk on the beach, she noticed something wasn't feeling well in her body. She sat down on a large rock to catch her breath.

Thoughts of what might be wrong flashed before her eyes and filled her head with terrible images. Without hesitation, she made her way back to the house. She asked

Maria, her housekeeper, who had taken care of her for the past 18 years, to call her doctor and arrange a visit to see him today. "I need to visit him today as soon as he can see me."

"What's the matter?" She asked.

"I'm not feeling myself. Just call him for me, please. I really don't feel like speculating on what might be or not."

Walking into her room seemed like an effort, and all she wanted to do was take a nap, but it was time for breakfast with Brian.

Grandma Kathrine could hear him washing up in the bathroom. The last thing she wanted him to know was that she was not feeling well. It was still and quiet this time but in an entirely different way. She changed into a casual dress for breakfast. Maria had prepared a full breakfast with eggs, bacon, fruit, and a fresh pot of coffee for the two of them to enjoy out by the patio overlooking the beach.

"Good morning, Brian. How did you sleep?"

"Good morning, Grandma. I slept so well last night. I left the window open next to my bed and listened to the sounds of the ocean all night. I can see why you love living here."

"I couldn't imagine living anywhere else," she responded. "Do you have an appetite this morning because Maria has cooked us a full breakfast?"

"Something about being by the water stimulates my appetite," he replied.

"Great. Let's have some coffee and begin where we left off last night with my storytelling."

He looked thrilled with the idea of continuing. "Sounds great, Grandma. Are you up to it?"

"Of course, I have never felt better." Now, this was so far from the truth; however, not to alarm Brian about just how serious the situation might be with her health, she smiled at him and drank a sip of her coffee. "Where was I anyway in the story?"

"You had just finished telling me about your date with Buttons."

Reflecting on that moment in her life, Grandma Kathrine had excitement in her voice. "Yes, exactly! It was love on every level with him."

As she stared at the ocean, a smile appeared across her face.

***

He made me feel so young and full of hope that I could find myself falling madly in love with him. However, I also found myself falling in love with the

Baron. As luck would have it, the Baron called me with his itinerary for New York. "Hello, Darling! I will be arriving on Friday for ten days. Does this schedule work for you?"

"Yes, darling, this will be perfect for me. I would like to meet you at the airport with the driver from St. Regis."

He answered with love in his voice, "See you in a couple of days. Goodbye, darling, I miss you."

"Goodbye, sweetheart. See you in two days."

The Baron arrived at JFK on a beautiful, hot August day. I was waiting for his arrival with anticipation when I spotted him walking down the ramp at the airport. The driver from St. Regis stood beside me, waiting for him to collect his bags and drive us into the city. His excitement to see me was overwhelming initially, but memories of our holiday in St. Tropez flashed through my mind and heart. We embraced one another with such passion and desire for each other. The time spent away from each other seemed like an eternity, and with the time away, the feeling became stronger. "Welcome to New York, darling."

His biggest smile was filled with a heartfelt appreciation that could be felt from within my heart. "I am so happy to finally be here with you, my darling." I felt connected to him again at that moment.

The desire to become close to this man became infinite for me. Our love affair had just begun to flourish, and with a little luck, it would grow into a true fairy tale. So, off to St. Regis, we all went with a glass of champagne in hand. The driver had it prepared to pour before we took off. "A toast to my New York adventures, with my darling beside me." We glanced at one another, toasted our glasses, and then drank our first of many glasses of champagne.

"This is for us and our love affair," I mentioned this because I felt like all of this was merely a dream.

He kissed me on the cheek to confirm my sentiments. As we enjoyed the ride into the city, I listened to The Baron ask the driver many questions about the city. He was filled with intrigue and curiosity about New York City. "Darling, I want to take you shopping for a new piece of jewelry from Cartier when we arrive at the Hotel."

I didn't see a problem with that request. "We can walk there from the Hotel."

Delighted with excitement to begin the love story with a touch of magic, we dropped his bags off with the doormen and walked down Fifth Avenue to Cartier. Walking through the front doors of Cartier, the Baron had in mind exactly the pieces of jewelry he wanted to see on me. A beautiful woman approached us, saying, "Hello, Sir. May I help you find something special?"

"Yes, could you please show my darling the new Fall Collection rings and bracelets?"

She jumped at the chance to make a sale for the Baron.

After trying on several rings and bracelets, the selection was narrowed down to two rings and matching bracelets. "Darling, which one do you like?" with a big smile.

"I really love these pieces."

He told the beautiful woman helping us, "We will take them."

"Perfect selection."

Within a few minutes, it was boxed and ready to go. We were thinking about having another glass of champagne to celebrate. "Let's walk back to our hotel and arrange with the concierge for dinner; then, we can have a glass of champagne in the Hotel Bar."

"Great idea, darling."

Before we had that drink and after we made dinner plans, we went up to our room to check it out.

A beautiful suite with all the bells and whistles, a room fit for a princess, and that was exactly how I felt at that moment. An American Princess in New York. I walked into the bedroom, where the closet door was slightly opened. I looked in, out of curiosity, at a full closet full of clothes. The Baron had arranged for a personal shopper to purchase clothes for me. "Sweetheart, whose clothes are these?"

"Darling, do you like them? I bought them for you based on what I thought you might love. I thought that we wouldn't have to run out this evening and purchase a dress for dinner."

The most elegant designer dresses were all my size.

Also, outfits for sightseeing and having lunch at the finest Restaurants in the city. Shoes to match everything. How could I not love them? A true fantasy of mine had just been fulfilled. "I am such a lucky girl to have met my Prince Charming."

He smiled with an appreciation for the finer things. He really got a thrill out of me dancing around like it was Christmas Day. "Shall we go have that glass of champagne, darling?"

"Maybe we could just have them delivered to us here in the room so I can start getting ready."

Quickly checking the kitchen bar area, only to realize we were set. They had chilled a bottle of the finest champagne for us. Opening the bottle and pouring two glasses for us, we then toasted to each other.

"Live like there's no tomorrow, love like it's your only day, and play along the way." These words slipped out of my mouth with true conviction. I believed them with every fiber within me. "Perfect, Darling...perfect." I kissed him and headed to the bathroom to prepare my bath. I couldn't wait to bathe in the most elegant bathtub I had ever seen.

Knowing all I needed was 30 minutes to look my best; I slipped into one of those designer dresses and matching shoes. The reservations for dinner were at 8 p.m. The Hotel had a driver waiting for us. When we arrived, the atmosphere was spectacular, with a view of all of Manhattan, which was charismatic enough to allure one's attention. My heart overflowed with love and gratitude as I turned to face the elegant man admiring me across the table. "Darling, you look so beautiful in your new dress and gorgeous jewelry this evening. How are you feeling?"

I thought to myself, how could I answer him without crying? "I feel like a Princess in a movie. Now I know how Grace Kelly must have felt in her fairy tale life." Knowing that it wasn't exactly the same, but to me, it was magical. I had to keep reminding myself that this was real and I wasn't dreaming of this lifestyle. We both enjoyed the wine, food, and company tremendously that evening. It reminded me of the first dinner we had together. The energy between us could be felt all around us. Not shy about drinking, we finished a bottle of wine together and decided to have another Champagne while deciding where to go next. "I feel a bit tired from my trip over, so would you mind if we could just go back to the hotel and have a nightcap there?"

The driver dropped us off in front of the hotel. While we proceeded to walk through the revolving doors, my eyes looked over to the other side, and a famous Rock star smiled at me with so much affection that it stopped me in my tracks. The greatest city in the world to connect with someone. We decided to just go up to our room and have that last drink, as if either one of us needed another one. "Let's have one more drink, Darling."

"No problem."

We began kissing each other in the doorway as we entered our room.

"I cannot wait to make love with you."

Chapter Six

The morning arrived with the most beautiful sunrise coming through the curtain into the room and beaming rays straight into my eyes. Those were the love rays that beamed through the room, filling it with lots of affection. "Good morning, darling." The first words that I heard filled my heart with so much love. The kind of love the world could feel.

"Good morning, sweetie," I said.

"Let's order some coffee," he suggested.

"I am a step ahead of you, my darling. It is waiting for you in the other room."

"Now I could wake up and start my day," he said.

We had planned so many fun adventures for the day that life was waiting to happen. First, we had coffee in the room, and then we would have breakfast downstairs. I wanted to show the Baron the sights of New York today. "Let's go see the Empire State Building, then go up to the Metropolitan Museum for the afternoon."

An excellent program for a beautiful August day that made me feel like a proper tourist in Manhattan. "Darling, I'm going to get ready now so we can get started on our day." Knowing I needed to jump up and start getting ready, I wasted no time.

After getting ready, we made our way downstairs for breakfast. As we walked down the hallway to catch the elevator, I said, "I am so excited to show you this wonderful city." Looking at the Baron with sheer pleasure, I explained to him the itinerary I had in mind for the day. He was thrilled to start our day with a tour of the top of the Empire State Building. "I've always dreamed of sharing this with someone I love."

We had a quick breakfast and went off to begin the day. It was a clear day with perfect visibility to see for miles around. While walking down Fifth Avenue to the Empire State Building, the Baron suggested grabbing a drink before going up to the top. "Darling, let's get a cold cocktail to enjoy the height. I have a bit of fear up there."

"I know that there is a place to get a drink at the top."

"PERFECT."

As we stood in line waiting to take the elevator to the top floor, I had so many ideas of places to show him after we finished there.

Once we reached the top, the view was

extraordinarily magnificent. "Would you like a cold beer, darling?" he asked.

"I would love one," I replied, though I wasn't much of a beer drinker, and neither was the Baron. But this occasion called for it—a moment to toast to with a cold beer and a cigarette.

"Here's to feeling on top of the world," he said as we clinked our bottles.

Taking a sip of beer, I gazed out at the vast landscape stretching for miles beyond the horizon. "It's a beautiful day for this kind of adventure," I remarked.

The Baron smiled at me, appreciating our moment atop the Empire State Building. "I've never been happier, higher, or more in love than I am with you at this moment in life. The precious gifts are right here. I feel God's presence surrounding us from up above."

All I could do was smile back at him, feeling the warmth of his words in my heart. I wanted to capture this moment forever, so I took a mental picture. Then, I approached a friendly tourist standing nearby and asked if they would kindly take our photo—a memory that would forever stay with me.

"Darling, should we venture off this platform and head down to visit the Metropolitan Museum?" I

suggested it, eager to continue exploring the city with the Baron.

With sheer delight, we made a move off the Empire State Building and caught a cab uptown. Before we reached 58th Street, the Baron asked me if I needed anything from any of the stores before we toured the Museum. "Darling, is there anything you need for this evening?" "No, sweetheart, I've arranged everything with the Concierge to purchase items for me." He seemed content with my reply. "Perfect." As we drove up to the museum, thoughts of what Buttons might have been up to on this glorious afternoon entered my mind. I couldn't help thinking of him. Once we entered the lobby, I could only think of taking in some culture for my soul. I needed beauty for the mind and for my soul to be nurtured on every level. "Where would you like to start, Darling?"

"At the bar, then off to the Impressionists of Modern Europe."

I knew an education was about to happen for me, and while the Baron explained each Artist in great detail to me, I was conscious of his knowledge, and his power excited me with each word delivered. His passion for culture astonished me. After an hour of walking through the museum and viewing each painting, we found our way out easily. "Thank you for the most enjoyable afternoon that I've ever encountered at the Museum."

The Baron replied, "It's my pleasure to fascinate a true believer. Should we hail a cab back to St. Regis and prepare for the evening?"

"Sounds like a plan."

Walking through the foyer at the St. Regis, the concierge approached us to confirm the plans for the evening. "Good evening. I have reserved the best table at Le Cirque for two. Would you like to have drinks before somewhere?"

"We will have drinks here, and then, if you could have our driver prepared to drive us over to the restaurant, we will have drinks there as well."

"Yes indeed."

We caught the elevator up to the room and organized an hour-long massage for two before getting ready for the evening.

That was exactly what the doctor ordered to relax and calm the body after a long day. After enjoying the massage, I prepared the bath with extra-special bubbles and bath beads. I had planned to wear an evening dress with beaded shoes and a bag to match. A picture of elegance walked through the door to model the dress for the Baron. *"Darling, you look so beautiful this evening,"* he said.

"I hope you approve," I replied back.

"Approve? I am speechless by your beauty. I would like to just marvel at you for a moment if you wouldn't mind. May I take a photo of you?"

"Please do, darling," I said with a smile. *"Shall we go have a drink of champagne downstairs?"*

"Absolutely."

"May I have a kiss to begin our evening?"

We embraced each other with so much passion. "Let's go to the bar, darling." Then, we went off to the bar for two glasses of champagne. After enjoying the drink, we jumped into the Town Car with our favorite driver. "Good evening, kids. How was your day spent here in New York City?"

His question received a casual response, "I have never been so in love with someone in my whole life. We are having the happiest time of our lives, acting like two big kids on holiday."

"PERFECT."

"This city tends to do that to everyone. May I add, Madam, that you look beautiful this evening?"

We touched each other behind the driver. It was hard to resist the affection for one another. "May I suggest the Sea Bass, as it is one of my favorites?" The driver smiled with strong approval.

"Sounds like a winner. I might just have that, and I'll let you know when I see you later."

"Perfect, I'll wait for you both." He jumped out to open the door for us to exit. "Enjoy these precious moments together, for we don't know what will happen tomorrow. Just live in the moment, feel the love for each other, and never let it go."

We both turned to him and smiled. We both could feel how special this moment was for each other. The heart lets love in on its own time, and time has no resistance.

Chapter Seven

Once comfortably seated in the finest spot within the restaurant, the waiter asked, "Good evening. May I start you off with two glasses of our finest champagne?" The Baron nodded to the waiter, signaling yes. As the waiter delicately placed the glasses on the table, we took no time in picking them and toasting to one another.

"To the woman who has my heart beating a different rhythm, and I love you for it," the Baron said, sealing the toast with a romantic kiss. Dinner went by quickly, with a bottle of wine and four glasses of champagne. The room had started spinning just a bit when I went to get up to leave.

"Darling, are you going to make it over there, or should I come around and help you?"

I assured him, "I'm fine, just fine, and darling. Where are we going now?"

"Let's get in the car, and then we can decide."

The walk to the car seemed so far but yet so close. "Let's go to the Monkey Bar, which is around the corner from here." Both of us were feeling no pain and simply a purely sexual attraction for each other. I had the desire to dance all night. That loving feeling had come over me, too, which many found stimulating. The guy on the piano became a good friend and always entertained me. I danced and sang with the Baron until it was time to go. He leaned over the piano and requested our favorite song, "It had to be you," We sang off-key and had no business singing at all. However, no one stopped us. When we decided to leave the bar, our driver had the door open and ready for us to depart. All I had on my mind was crawling into bed. The alcohol consumption had taken over at that point in the evening, and without a doubt, it was time to crash. "Darling, take a sleeping pill of mine. It will help with the hangover in the morning." I wasn't sure what he was handing me, but I took it anyway. It was only half a pill, which made for sticky fingers handling it.

"What kind of pill is this, darling?" speaking from an intoxicating level of existence.

"Darling, you will feel much better in the morning. Just sleep now, and we will continue the celebration in the morning.

"Goodnight, darling."

I had no clue what kind of pill this was. I

swallowed, but it helped me sleep and feel fine in the morning. I am guessing it was also the 9 hours of sleep.

Awakening to a sunny, new day in New York City allows you to pretend even the best tourist has nothing on you. I had planned each day meticulously for our time spent in New York. The agenda for the day was shopping and lunch with Carol. She was watching my two toy poodles while the Baron spent the week here.

The morning started slowly, with breakfast in the room and reading the paper in our bathrobes. "Darling, how are you feeling this morning?"

"I am feeling like a young girl in love for the first time."

The response surprised him. "I would like to get ready quickly so we can walk over to Park Avenue, where a surprise awaits you."

I responded without hesitation, "What kind of surprise, darling?"

"You will see just as soon as you get dressed for the day."

Wondering what the surprise could be, I jumped up and began to prepare my bath.

A stunning feeling came over my entire body, filled with desire and passion for this man. I had never been treated like this before and, without a doubt, knew that this experience might be once in a lifetime. Embrace it, enjoy it, and live it. I got dressed and was ready to walk out the door within thirty minutes, and I could feel the Baron beginning to get excited about something. I'm not sure of the reason, but I knew in my heart that this surprise would delight me. As we walked to meet the elevator doors, I glanced at his face and felt pure excitement coming from his heart. "Darling, I have never seen you act so happy."

He stared into my eyes with complete compassion. "I have never loved anyone as much as I love you, darling." The elevator doors opened to the lobby, and we walked towards the revolving doors. Once we walked through them, the Baron directed me to turn right and walk toward Park Avenue. At this point, the suspense was killing me. He gently took my hand and opened the door to the BMW showroom. "I need to order a part for my car back in Belgium, darling. Why don't you have a look around?"

"I will, darling."

Before you can really look around, you have to imagine actually owning one and driving it off the showroom floor. This is where I began to observe the cars displayed in the showroom in detail.

I walked up to the most exciting of all the cars, the convertible. I opened the door and climbed into this beautiful car. The beige leather interior and open space invited me to test drive it. Looking in the rear-view mirror, I noticed the Baron looking at me like a salesman. "Darling, do you like this one?"

"I absolutely love this one."

"Do you like the exterior color?"

Looking around at the outside of this car, I connected with this green BMW. I could actually see myself driving this car down the street.

"Darling, this car is yours. I just bought it for you, and you can drive it off the showroom in two days."
"What??? I didn't hear you?"

*He repeated himself, "I bought this car for you, my love. **It's YOUR CAR.**"*

The room expanded in my mind by about the length of a football field, and the excitement level could be felt throughout the dealership. The feeling of someone's wish coming true on National Television consumed the energy in the room. "I am the happiest girl in the world, sweetheart. This is perfect timing for the upcoming trip with my family to Maine."

"That was my incentive to buy it today. Knowing that you needed a car on Friday, I decided to buy you one. All of this is because I love you, darling."

"Let's go for lunch at Cipriani's."

"Perfect place to celebrate, darling." I kissed him with an appreciation for how much I loved him.

"Shall we go enjoy the experience, darling?" He asked with a sweet voice. "I am so excited about all of this happening so fast."

I needed a Bellini from Cipriani's. Carol was at the bar with three drinks waiting for us. "Hello, you two lovebirds."

So many amazing adventures, enlightened experiences, and love from a different perspective filled my heart during this part of my life.

***

Grandma Kathrine wasn't sure if Brian could understand this concept of her script, except that he was mature and wise enough to convince her how similar they were.

"What you must have been going through at this time," said Brian as he soaked in her story.

Maria interrupted, "Can I get you both anything before we have to leave for the Doctor?"

"What time do I need to be ready, Maria?"

Looking down at her watch and up again, she said, "In an hour."

"Would you like to come, Brian?" Grandma Kathrine asked.

"Sounds like a plan," he responded with some reservations and gave a small but gentle smile. He wondered what the visit might be about and if anything was troubling his grandmother.

"Let's go, gang," sparked Henry's amusement.

They all headed for the car in the garage. Henry opened the door for the ladies while Brian helped himself to the backseat.

"Everyone in and ready to go? Let's roll, Henry."

Brian thought his grandmother had a unique way of connecting with everyone compassionately and loving all without judgment. She was an amazing spiritual being able to personalize each situation with humor. The way she handled pain and suffering reminded you of a great warrior. As Brian reflected on her legacy, he realized that this would be the moment that this testimony would ring true for her.

The doctor called her in to run more tests to see exactly what problem she had discovered on that morning walk. After the tests were all taken and she was discharged, she met someone at the front desk who would shed some light on the problem. A nurse from behind the desk jumped up to greet everyone. "I have a few words of wisdom from experience. I have seen charts like yours before, and it can be a simple procedure that would take minimal recovery time."

Everyone looked at each other curiously as to exactly what she was referring to.

"All indications point to needing a Kidney Transplant."

Everyone processed this for a moment with such concern for what would follow. They all headed towards the car in the parking garage. No one said a word to each other.

"I feel like having lunch at the beach," said Grandma Kathrine.

Brian knew that his grandmother possessed an incredible knack for making serious situations light and calm. This was evident to him by the way she lived her life. Brian began to reflect on the life she had led and all the abuse she had done to her body through the years of drinking, smoking, and other choices that she had made. Brian knew she had to come clean about what had caused this problem and what solutions she had to take to resolve it. The laughter among everyone broke the silence. Henry drove the car towards the beach and to her favorite French Café adjacent to the beach.

"I feel like a real French experience," Grandma Kathrine said with a French accent.

Once in the restaurant, she requested a table outside facing the ocean.

"Where was I in my story?"

Everyone could feel her urgent energy mixed with her desire to finish telling the most beautiful love story in detail. Without further ado, she dived in.

***

The last night of the Baron's first visit to NYC was spent enjoying time together and planning my first trip to Belgium.

"Darling, after you spend time with your family in Maine, I would like to have you fly to Belgium to experience my world with me."

All I could think of at that moment was spending a fabulous time learning and living his life as best as he could.

"I will arrange everything with Sylvia; she takes care of all my travel plans. I will have her send you an itinerary."

I was overwhelmed with excitement and jumped up and hugged him from across the table. I knew our love for each other would continue to grow stronger with time, and sharing time with him in Belgium felt like the next adventure. We enjoyed the fine wine and spectacular cuisine in a favorite spot we had already experienced. Our eyes were fixated on each other's love for each other. "Darling, I will miss you until we are together again. I have had the most wonderful holiday with you and wish to spend every minute with you." A tender moment of being in appreciation for the other.

"I have enjoyed having you here in New York, where I could share a part of my world with you."

Both raised their wine glasses together to acknowledge the moment spent behind them and toast to their next moment together.

"Until we meet again."

With a smile and a kiss, we toasted one another. That night ended on such a beautiful note. The next day, the flight departed at noon. "Goodbye, darling; I'll call you when I arrive home. Thank you again for a spectacular time. Take care of yourself, and know that I miss you already."

I knew the feelings were mutual between us. "I will miss you, darling."

As the embrace between us seemed like an eternity, the driver started the car in front of the hotel. Meanwhile, we parted only to smile at each other with love and compassion for each other.

I watched the car drive off, wondering when we would be together again. The plans were to meet up in two weeks after spending a week in Maine with my family, celebrating my parent's wedding anniversary. The house I rented was on the Maine coast, with nine bedrooms and views from every window of the water for the family to relax and enjoy their time together. I was packed and ready to pick up the new BMW convertible. Then, I began the journey to pick up my grandfather for the family reunion in Maine.

As I made my way to the BMW dealership, my heart pounded with excitement. Arriving with total excitement for my new car, I jumped out of the cab and ran to the door to see my new car waiting for me.

"May I help you with something?" asked a salesman.

"I'm here to pick up my new car. It's that convertible over there."

I walked up to my new car, and the salesman gave me the information before handing me the keys. As I drove the car out onto the open road, I felt a sense of freedom and independence that I had never experienced before.

The wind rushed through my hair, the sun on my face, and the sound of the engine roaring beneath me was all so exhilarating. While enjoying the drive out of Manhattan and up to Vermont, time flew by with every mile. My anticipation of seeing Grandpa brought back memories of my childhood with him. He lived with our family for six months out of the year and the other six months in Vermont for most of my childhood. The fondest memories had Grandpa always attached to them.

Chapter Eight

Driving with plenty of daylight left, I headed towards Grandpa's residence to retrieve him for the family reunion in Maine. A milestone for the family and a reason for celebration, filled with laughter, hugs, and memories that cannot be matched with any other warmth and comfort. As I pulled into the parking lot, I drove up to his apartment, and there he was, waiting for me, with his head peeking out of his curtains.

He came to the door and greeted me with lots of hugs. "Hey, Little Kathrine, how are you?" with a thrill of excitement in his voice to finally be there.

I answered, "I'm just so happy to see you, Gramps. How are you feeling?"

"I'm doing fine. Ready for this trip to Maine. When is your father getting there?"

"Today, Gramps, today. Let's get your things and be on our way."

"Sounds good, sweetheart. I've been ready to go since yesterday."

"Let's Roll Tide."

Packed up and ready to roll, we checked his apartment one last time to make sure he had all his things.

While driving up Route 30 to Maine, we decided to have lunch at the Dorset Inn, which once belonged to his aunt Amey. His summers were spent there, helping her out and having fun as a young man. This would be a perfect place to connect with him through the memories of his family.

The conversation between us seemed timeless. Stories of yesterday's memories flooded his thought process, and it made for a swift trip. The dogs were with us but never bothered us the entire trip. Once we arrived at the house, we drove up the long driveway to the big house by the sea.

An unbelievable old Captain's House with views directly to the ocean. A picture-perfect retreat house for the family to celebrate the 30th wedding anniversary of Dad and Mom. "Grandpa, how do you like the house?"

Without hesitation, he replied, "This is some place for all of us to be together."

I could feel peace from within his soul. This place would mean so much to him and our family. The memories of summers spent in Maine began with his childhood and were passed on to his son and then to all of us. I knew this would be one of those moments in life that captures your heart and makes you feel young again. This inspired me to make it the best trip ever. Just at that moment, Dad and Mom, along with the brothers, drove into the driveway.

"Welcome to Maine, guys."

As they began to look around at the place, a connection between all of us happened. Time stood still for that moment with us. As I made eye contact with my father, I could feel his heart filled with much love and happiness. He felt at home in Maine.

"Let's go get some steamers and a fresh lobster." The music playing throughout the house had us feeling alive, and with the windows open, the fresh air from the ocean fragranced each room.

"I'm ready; let's go. I'll drive my new car for everyone to enjoy with the top down."

The weather was ideal for a drive in a convertible. The sun peeked over the horizon, casting a warm glow across the ocean. The water glistened in the light, creating a mesmerizing effect. The air was crisp and refreshing, with a gentle breeze blowing on our faces.

The fresh smell of balsam pine trees with ocean views made for a drive I would never forget. It was one of those days you could appreciate knowing that this memory would never come again. I pulled up to the Pier and parked the car close to the fresh lobster tanks. You could see the steam coming off the pots in the kitchen. "I will order for us; you guys find the perfect seat," Dad ordered for the gang while we strolled along the pier, looking for the perfect table.

A waitress came up to us and took our drink order.

We decided to order a bottle of rose wine and a couple of beers for the guys. As the drinks arrived, the food followed suit. "What a delicious feast this is for our family." Everyone lifted their glasses and cheered for the family. A fantastic holiday spent with family and a beautiful memory in the making

A full week of family fun in Maine, with everyone contributing their part to the memories. Mornings were filled with fresh blueberry picking and strolls along the Ocean, followed by afternoon naps in a hammock overlooking the Ocean. Then, a game of tennis to end the day. At sunset, everyone met on the wrap-around terrace for cocktails. Dinner with the family always consisted of laughter for hours. There was never a shortage of laughter with the brothers on hand. Days turned into nights, and the two weeks spent with everyone were beautiful moments. It was a reminder of how beautiful the world can be when family is around.

Fresh seafood and long walks through the pine-scented trails along the Maine coast added a dimension of spirituality to our souls. We always gave back what we received from our Maine experience. The moments shared together would be remembered years from now, so we all just basked in the moment. The thought of leaving this happy place saddened me to no end. I knew this time would never come again for me, and I relived each scene like a movie on any given day.

The time had come to make plans to travel to Boston on my way home to New York. I had been in conversation with Buttons while in Maine. We had made plans to spend time together at his father's home in Boston for the weekend. I was ready for that adventure with Buttons, but I wasn't sure what I was in for with his family. I knew in my heart that he was in my life for so many reasons that they would present themselves one day. So, for now, just enjoy the experiences and allow life to happen.

Pulling into Boston felt like a new experience for me. It had been so many years since I had visited Boston. As I exited the Highway, I had a nervous feeling stuck in my stomach. The kind of feeling you get before you jump out of a plane or begin a new relationship with your heart. The heart lets love in without warning.

The perfect day for driving a Convertible, with the coolness of an August day in New England and not a cloud in the sky, made for an enjoyable ride. While looking for the exact address, I received a phone call from Buttons. "Hey you, where are you?"

I answered him back, "I just arrived at your street." "My father has left a sign on the door for you, but I am at my cousin's Wedding. Go ahead, and I'll meet up with you after this is over."

"No problem. See you soon!"

I was unsure what house to look for except one with a note taped to the front door. I thought to myself, "How difficult could this be, for God's sake?"

I could feel my heart beating extra fast as I turned down the street in search of the door with a note attached to it. Halfway down the street, I turned to my left side, and there it was, "New York, come on in."

Just as big as the smile on my face, the letters seemed to jump off the paper away from the door and into my heart.

I could feel so much passion from this note taped to the front door as I pulled into his driveway. I knew that the people you meet in your life would affect you somehow, but at that moment, I just didn't know the extent of our relationship yet. What I did know to be true were my feelings for Buttons. I opened the door to find the lights on and a bottle of wine placed on the table with a note, "Welcome and make yourself at home. Please pour a glass of wine, and we will be home soon." I helped myself to a glass or two before they arrived. I looked around the house, where family photos filled the walls of hallways on both sides. His mother was a very beautiful woman who died way too early in her life.

***

While having lunch on the beach, everyone was engaged with the story.

"What was your feeling at that moment towards the Baron?" Brian asked.

"Not sure. At that point, I felt a very strong bond between Buttons and me."

As they finished lunch and paid the bill, it was off for a drive along the ocean on the most beautiful Spring Day. One of those days that inspires you to do something crazy.

"Let's go for a swim at the beach. Who's up for going with me?"

Brian saw that his grandma had gotten wild hair after telling her story of that exact moment when she knew she was in love with Buttons.

All those feelings from that memory were alive again for her, Brian thought and said, "I'll go with you, Grandma."

"Henry, please drop us off at the lobby so we can go up and get our bathing suits, then park the car and grab your camera so you can take pictures of Brian and me swimming. I want to capture this precious memory for Brian."

After swimming with such pleasure, they watched the sunset from the beach together. The colors in the sky were so bright, with so much love and passion. A perfect way to end the day with her grandson. This moment would never be forgotten, even with time. "I am so proud of you, Brian, for all that you have become in your life. I see your grandfather in your eyes. Remember this for the rest of your life: **You are loved**."

A silence between the two of them lasted an eternity in her mind as she reached for his hand. She knew this love would continue to shine because it's been passed down through the generations. "Promise me that when you find that perfect girl you want to tell this story to, she will deserve your love."

"I promise, Grandmother, that the girl of my dreams will be worthy of my love."

A nip in the air caused a change in location. Henry strolled down to the beach to check on them and ask if they needed anything. "You two enjoying the sunset?"

"Oh yes, Henry, my grandson and I have had an amazing time together. We are coming to the Condo now because it's getting cool out here."

"Will you continue on with your love story, Grandmother?"

"Of course I will, sweetheart... Where was I in my story? Oh yes, I'm preparing to travel to Belgium for the first time."

Chapter Nine

The Baron had scheduled my flight to leave on a Friday evening, putting me there around mid-morning the following day. The excitement level of the unknown thrilled me without question. "Do I seriously want this?" I decided to put my mind at ease and arrived at JFK early to check-in. Not sure what to bring with me, I packed enough to get me through the first couple of days. Shopping in Belgium would be first on the list of things to do. After I checked in, I headed to the lounge for first-class passengers.

I ordered wine and a cheese plate while waiting for my flight. I made phone calls to family and friends to let everyone know that I was headed out of the Country for a week. This was something I did before every trip. As the phone rang, I noticed the Baron was calling me.

"Hello, Darling, how are you?"

"Hello, my sweet darling. Are you ready to board your flight to come to see me?"

"I am ready to be there with you, sweetheart." Without hesitation, he replied, "I'll be there to receive you, my darling, Bisou Bisou."

I heard my flight being announced over the loudspeaker and realized I needed to make my way to the gate. "Darling, I'll see you very soon, my love."

"I'll be there to receive you, darling."

As we said goodbye to one another, I could feel my soul connecting to this man's heart completely. And with that thought, I was off to Belgium for the experience of a lifetime.

The next day I arrived with such anticipation to greet the Baron and be back in his arms. Making my way through customs, I finally saw him. He was waving to me from the window, the last step before freedom.

"Darling, it's really you. Welcome to my Country."

As we embraced each other, I was relieved that this moment had finally arrived. The journey of our love story began with the same smiles we were giving each other at that moment, and while I felt so much love for him, I could also feel some for myself. "Let's go have some lunch with my friends Lauren and Sylvia, the girls that were with us in St. Tropez that sunny day by the beach."

"Fantastic, darling. I am looking forward to reconnecting with them here in Belgium."

As his driver took my bags from baggage claim, we all headed towards the front door, where the car was parked along the curbside for easy access. "Darling, I am so happy you are here with me without a moment to spare. Let's have a glass of Champagne here in the car."

The driver had arranged for this moment ahead of time. The cork was slightly opened, allowing the Baron to open it with ease. "To my darling, I am so happy you're finally here. We are going to have a beautiful week." Toasting our Champagne glasses together with love in our eyes while looking into the others, a magical feeling came over me. I knew we both felt that magic at the same time.

"I would like to say something now to my sweetheart. I am so happy to be here with you and look forward to an outstanding week."

The love in the car had the driver smiling from ear to ear. We were off to the restaurant to meet the girls, along with the Baron's best friend, David. He was his banker and best friend, too. This was new territory for me to experience with him. Being introduced to his world meant having an open mind to what they might think of us together.

His confidence level was strong with all the love coming from him, and the true test was about to begin as we pulled up to the restaurant. A charming French Bistro set the perfect ambiance for a reunion with Lauren and Sylvia. Walking into the restaurant, I felt utterly serene about meeting his friends. I knew this moment would be enjoyable for all of us. His friend David graciously flagged us over to the table where they had already been seated.

"Bonjour." He introduced me to David with so much love in his heart. "This is my beautiful Darling that I have been raving about to you."

"Welcome; it's so nice to finally meet you."

I looked over to the girls I had met in the South of France and approached them with a hug and kiss. "It's so great to see you both again. Everything going well?"

They answered me one at a time, "Yes, all is well with us. How was your flight over from New York?"

"It was a long but easy flight; I slept most of the trip."

Then, the Baron joined me in the conversation, saying, "I am so happy that my darling is here with me." He leaned over and gave me a big kiss. "Let's toast to the happiness within all of us and the feeling I have for my darling. Cheers to everyone!"

The mood among everyone seemed upbeat without hesitation, and the Baron ordered several bottles of wine for the table. I began to notice that this was something he enjoyed doing for his friends. The lunch went off without a hitch. After enjoying several bottles of wine and a three-course lunch, this was the determining factor. Laughter consumed the table with stories from our St. Tropez trip. The Baron was animated in his storytelling and loved hitting the high points. I felt a bit jet-lagged and exhausted, so with the intention of taking a nap, I asked if we could leave soon. "I'll get the bill from the waiter and call our driver to pick us up."

I whispered to the Baron, "I hope you're okay with leaving, darling; I feel a bit tired from my trip and the wine."

"No problem, darling."

We told everyone goodbye for the moment. The attention placed on my arrival was overwhelming, to say the least. On the drive home, we stopped off to pick up Opera tickets for this evening's performance. All I could think of at that moment was a pillow and a bed.

"Darling, you go ahead, and I'll tend to your luggage."

Walking into his home, I was greeted by Marian, his housekeeper, who took care of everything. "Bonjour," I answered, "Hello, I am so happy to be here but extremely fatigued now, so could you be as kind as to show me to my room?"

She began walking up the stairs and turned on the light in the Baron's room.

She was showing me where to put my things just before I collapsed in front of her. "Merci Beaucoup." She turned around and headed out towards the staircase. "Darling, are you up there?" I could hear the Baron's voice from downstairs, ringing in my ear. I knew that if I didn't lie down right now, he could forget about me going tonight. "Yes, dear, I am up here getting ready to lay down."

He walked into the bathroom, where I was washing my face and preparing to nap for an hour or two. "You get some rest, my love, and when you awake, we will arrange for the driver to take us for dinner before the Opera. I will show you around my home later."

Finally, I could be horizontal after traveling from New York, having lunch with new friends, and having two bottles of wine. "I am going to rest now, darling. Wake me in an hour or two if I am not up."

After awakening from a long nap, I jumped up and showered to be ready for the evening. "Darling, may I bring you a glass of Champagne while you get ready?" "Yes, please." I would never say no to that request. Later, I dressed and got ready to go. I walked downstairs to the sitting room, where Baron greeted me. "Darling, I have a gift for you. A little something to remember this evening." He handed me a small box with a big ribbon attached to it. Opening it with amazement, I slowly lifted the top of the box up and saw a stunning diamond and sapphire necklace. "Oh, my word, darling, this is such a magnificent piece." "Do you like it, darling? Let me put it on you."

"Wow! This is some necklace, sweetheart."

"A gift to my love on our first date in Belgium."

The time had come for us to leave for dinner and then the Opera. "Shall we go, darling?"

The driver had been waiting for us to proceed to the car. "Good evening," he said as he opened my door. I felt like a new experience was about to happen for me. I knew at that moment while sitting in the car that people come into your life to serve a purpose, teach a lesson, or help you figure out who you are or want to become in life.

For now, I knew just to enjoy this special relationship and treasure each moment. The car pulled up to a building that was luminous with the colors of the show we would attend. "Darling, we are here at the Opera House. We will be joining friends of mine for dinner inside, then up to our box seats to watch the show."

Once inside the Opera House, the energy felt so grand. A period in time that seemed alive again. People of all ages, races, and genders were promenading around. I was really taken aback by the Opera House's magnificence as soon as we entered. Thereafter, we stepped into the restaurant, where his friends had a table waiting for us. "Good evening. I would like to introduce my darling Kathrine from New York."

Everyone smiled with delight and introduced themselves one by one. After we took our seats, the Baron turned to me and said, "Shall we have champagne, darling?"

"Absolutely, sweetheart."

The waiter brought his finest bottle of vintage champagne to the table and, with a smile, poured the champagne into our glasses. We were ready for a toast. "May our love grow stronger and many returns to Belgium, darling." I smiled back at him and kissed him on the lips. "Thank you, sweetheart."

The waiters served us dinner while we listened to the Opera from a distance. Preparing us for the experience we were about to have in our box seats off the balcony. That was exactly what happened to us after enjoying dinner. The curtain went up, and for the next two hours, we were entertained by Angelic voices and movement. I glanced over at the Baron during the show, and I was received with a smile that hugged my heart with complete love. After the show, we said Goodnight to his friends and headed to the car. Once back at his house, we finished the night with a nightcap. "Darling, I hope you enjoyed this evening as much as I did. Being with you here in Belgium is such a wonderful experience for me. Make yourself at home here, darling."

"Thank you, darling. I am having the most incredible time with you here. Your friends are so beautiful and love you very much."

He leaned over and began to kiss me. I could feel his soul touching mine in a way I had never felt before this moment. Two lovers expressing their love for one another is an enlightening experience. Our passion for each other became stronger and deeper. The clothes started coming off without us realizing it, and we found ourselves walking up the staircase into his room. Candles had been lit by Marian, his housekeeper, before she retired to bed. The magic of love surrounded the room and added to the atmosphere of pure pleasure.

Making love to each other was sensual and sexy. Caressing went on till we both fell asleep with the music playing in the background. The morning was so peaceful, and Marian served breakfast when we decided to eat on the terrace. "Bonjour Cheri." The Baron kissed me and smiled at me with so much love from his heart. I knew this would be a fabulous day with all the love shining through my heart. "Darling, would you like to have our coffee on the terrace overlooking the city? I have a surprise trip planned for us, and I want to explain all the events we will be attending."

With one eye open and not feeling awake just yet, I knew he had taken the time to arrange this trip with so much compassion that I must be awake and prepared to indulge in excitement. "Yes, my love, let's take our coffee to the terrace, where we can discuss your plans for the day."

Once outside, I felt a moment of calm come over me. I believed this lifestyle was everything I had been dreaming of for myself. A fairytale life with all the elements: love, wealth, and prestige

"Darling, I have arranged for us to drive up to the Coast, where we can stay at my Cottage by the sea, but before that, I want to take you to an exhibit of Hans Memling, a very famous artist from our country. Then a beautiful lunch along the Ocean, just the two of us, followed by a short drive to my cottage, where we will have an amazing, sexy dinner with our clothes on."

I began to laugh after he delivered that last line. His sense of humor never disappointed me. "Sounds like a spectacular trip for us to get to know each other better. I will get ready and be back down, ready to go off on our adventure."

"Excellent, darling."

His excitement level could be felt while I prepared for the surprise trip. Finished and ready to head downstairs, I was met by the love of my life with a proposal on the staircase. "Have you ever felt this way about another man?"

"No, my love. This love is one of a kind."

He smiled and asked for my hand, where he placed a beautiful bracelet on my wrist. "This is a token of my love for you. I am crazy about you and plan to be with you forever." This made me smile all over with love that knows no boundaries. "You are one of a kind, my love. I am ready for our adventure."

"Then let's go explore our world along the coast." His driver was waiting for us to drive us up to Bruges, which would be a new experience for me. The views from my seat were spectacular. "I love you, darling." He smiled with a heart full of desire and passion for life.

"Darling, this exhibit we are heading to is celebrating the 500th anniversary of his death. His work is very famous all over the world. One of his most famous pieces, The Last Judgement, remains one of Memling's most masterful creations. It immediately set the tone for his spatial vision with its sense of the cosmic while creating a divine world of physical rather than hieratic dimensions. He was the painter of the dream. I hope you will enjoy his work as I do."

I loved his zest for culture, and his passion for educating me was so beautiful. I knew at this moment to absorb it all in, for there might not be a chance of such freedom to explore without restrictions. We engaged in every room with full appreciation for his work and creativity. I was blown away by his detail in creating a reality. The more I got into the piece, the more love I had for this man. Life was to be lived, and I felt that at this very moment, I was alive. "Let's go have lunch, darling. I have worked up an appetite with all this beauty."

We finished up with a kiss. The feeling between us grew stronger as we absorbed all that culture.

"I would like to have lunch at this famous restaurant, where the only thing on the menu is mussels and frites (French fries), which, come to find out, were originally from Belgium. I have worked up an appetite while observing the countryside of Belgium. Let's have lunch."

The driver turned off the highway and pulled up to the front door, where we were greeted by the valet boys. "Bonjour" back and forth greetings to all. While walking through the front door, the fragrance of fresh seafood and the savory flavors of different wine sauces embodied our walk to our table.

A view of the ocean from a window. "Merci" "Darling, this restaurant serves only mussels and French fries with the wine of your choice."

"Well, then, Rose, all day for me."

The Baron stimulated the conversation with his knowledge of life stories and world events. He proceeded to tell me about the saddest moment in his life. "Darling, I would like to share my family's story with you. It was the invasion of Belgium and the kidnapping of my father by the Nazis.

Our family wealth and all of our possessions were taken by Hitler and his men. We had so many beautiful pieces of art, only to be robbed of them by the enemy. My father was allowed to work but was then picked up and held hostage at night. This was a horrible time in my life."

"How did it all end?" A sadness came over him as he told me in detail about the events.

"The Nazis killed most of our friends and some family but spared us because of our name and family wealth. We offered them millions for our freedom."

I felt as if this was an extremely sensitive subject and one we should stop at for the moment. We needed some laughter at this moment, and not being too disrespectful; I mentioned that there was an exhibit in Belgium that explained in detail this crucial moment in history. "I read a full article in the paper over breakfast about this exhibit. Shall we go tomorrow?"

"I would love to show you this exhibit, my love, but first, a lunch fit for a Queen and a little shopping along the way."

What a day to indulge in true culture and fine cuisine! This made me feel like a true Baroness.

The experience of fresh mussels in a rose sauce could only be described as "Delicious." And indeed, it was delicious.

"Darling, thank you for educating me today on all things beautiful."

Without missing a beat, "Avec pleasure, Moi Cheri. This has been one of my favorite days of all time."

We enjoyed the last drop of our wine and went off to see the sights in town. Then, we walked into a little shop that sold unique items. "Please pick out something that will always remind you of this moment, darling."

I found a book on the exhibit that we had just explored. "This would be a perfect gift."

"Perfect, Darling."

We walked to the car and headed to his Cottage along the Ocean. At first glance, I couldn't believe that he didn't live here full-time. A big, beautiful home on the beach. "Welcome to my little home by the sea," said the

Baron.

"This is not a little home, sweetheart. A piece of paradise is more like how I would describe this place."

We opened the door to his cottage; all you could see were walls full of amazing art pieces. Most of them were priceless art pieces, which made me wonder why he wouldn't donate them to a museum. "Darling, these are just a few pieces that the Nazis returned to our family. We had so many that were never recovered from the Nazis."

A home full of history and timeless pieces. That's spectacular, I said to myself. He educated me on each one of them. This took all night and then some, but I was eager to learn. He poured us both a glass of wine, and we walked around the house. The music he had playing throughout the house was classical Opera.

An invitation to feel all the passion we had experienced in a day was almost overwhelming.

"Darling, what do you think about this piece? I want to ship it to our new condo in the sky and several other pieces. Which one would you like to have hung in our new home?"

I didn't know how to answer him because these pieces were so special and extremely expensive.

Chapter Ten

Grandma Kathrine was not sure what to say to Brian at this moment except, "That's when you know you've arrived at the door of love, and whether you walk in or just knock is up to you and where you are in your spiritual journey." She paused for a moment, as if to soak in the truth of her words.

"So, shall we go upstairs for a sunset cocktail? I'm ready for one after all this talk about love."

He looked at her with eyes full of curiosity as to what that moment meant to her.

"How did you feel about the Baron up to that point?"

"I found the whole experience a page out of a romantic novel. A new-found love within a body whose soul was connected to mine."

The music playing on the radio was from Grandma Kathrine's favorite jazz singer.

"I feel like opening a very good bottle of Italian Red Wine. Will you be joining me, Brian, with wine, or do you feel like something else?"

"I'll join you in having a glass of wine."

As Henry opened the wine, Grandma Kathrine felt the need to inspire Brian with thoughts from her life experiences.

"These quotes are from living a life full of love:
Take a chance on love, no matter how it may turn out.
Always know that you have the courage to experience a love that is strong and free and without regret.
Never forget the day your heart let love in forever.
Dreams of holding on to these feelings forever would present a lifetime of connection between soulmates."

With that, she paused as she looked at her grandson's face. "These passionate words must be a part of your thinking in life. What are you thinking, my beautiful grandson?"

Brian looked a bit confused with the secondaries written on his face. "How did you feel about your new love for the Baron?"

"I felt alive for the first time in my life and never wanted to leave that space. You know when it hits you that you have arrived home in your heart. Shall we have some dinner, Brian, or continue drinking our dinner tonight?"

With a cute chuckle, he answered me, "I just want you to finish telling me your beautiful story, so I'm not very hungry but sure could use another drink."

Holding his glass up, she reached over and filled it with more wine. "Well, there you have it. A man after my own heart. Without further delay, I must finish telling you how much compassion I had for the Baron at this point in my life."

"Have you always felt compassion for everyone in your life?"

"Yes, Brian. Anyone that has ever walked into my life has touched my heart with some form of love."

"Where was your heart with Buttons?"

"My heart was and will always be with this man. My awareness of his gift was not recognizable at first, but as time passed, I came to understand just how magical his gift was to me. One can come into your life at any given moment and never leave because you choose to let them stay for eternity. This was his gift."

Brian looked at his grandmother with so much love from his heart that she could feel the light from within shining so brightly. "What happened to the Baron?"

"Well, we had an unforgettable experience together while I was in Belgium for the first time, and now I had to return to New York."

***

It was September, and New York is such a beautiful city this time of year to enjoy the fall. Leaving the Baron was difficult, but knowing that we would be reunited in a couple of weeks for his Birthday in New York made it easier. He drove me to the airport around noon to catch an afternoon flight.

"Darling, I will miss your sweet voice and beautiful face. Until we meet again, darling, you must remember this: "It had to be you, my love."

This had become our song, and he would sing it to me. "I will keep you close to my heart, darling."

We kissed one another, and he whispered in my ear, "Till we meet again, darling."

I turned to him with a smile from my soul and then proceeded to walk to my gate. The journey home went rather quickly because of a long-overdue nap I enjoyed on my flight. When I arrived, the flight was touching down in New York. Still feeling asleep, I walked down to grab my bags at the baggage claim and hailed a cab to take me home. A video played in my head of all the beautiful memories I shared with the Baron and thoughts of our next adventure ending as the cab driver pulled up to my building. The simple luxury of being home seemed overwhelming at first, but then I settled in and thought of calling Buttons. I had missed his laugh and cute smile, not to mention his great personality.

After dialing his number, a sudden nervousness came over me.

He answered, "Hey there, beautiful, how are you?" I didn't know what to say except, "I'm great; how about yourself?"

We were flirting with each other because we could. "When can I see you again?"

I replied. "Me?"

"Dinner tomorrow night around 8 p.m."

I quickly answered, "Yes, let's have dinner tomorrow night. I'll see you at 8 p.m."

I knew that dinner with him would be a 24-hour date consisting of dinner, dancing, a diner, and then romance. In that very order, I felt so sexy around him, but I knew that our love for each other would only develop with time.

I found myself thinking about the Baron; at other times, Buttons had been on my mind. I couldn't help but imagine both of them in my life. My heart was divided between two men at this point in my life, with no holding back or caution for the road ahead. The desires that came over me when I thought of Buttons kissing me excited me beyond my wildest dreams. I decided to call it a day after all my travels. I arranged a spa day with a facial, massage, manicure, pedicure, and Brazilian waxing.

After spending most of the day relaxing, I dashed home to get ready for my date with Buttons. I bought a new dress and lingerie for the occasion at my favorite boutique across the street from my apartment. Time was on my side; I still had plenty of time for a bubble bath with new oils. I prepared the bath and poured myself a glass of wine.

After enjoying my glass of wine while soaking, I reached for the towel and started lathering my body with essential oils, followed by cream. I wanted my body to be ready for whatever the evening brought my way. Dressed and ready to rock, the doorman buzzed me to announce my date's arrival. "Please let him know that I am coming down now." I grabbed my evening bag in one hand and lipstick in another, kissed the dogs, and went out the door. I went to meet Buttons downstairs. From a distance, I heard, hello, beautiful, and ran over to him and hugged his neck.

He kissed me and grabbed my hand. "I've missed you, beautiful."

I kissed him back without thinking twice and said, "I am so happy to be back in your arms."

That was another attraction I had toward him. He had the most muscular arms. He worked out every day, and you could tell from his body that he did. When we reconnected, it was surreal. When we smiled at one another, the love spell was cast for us. We hailed a cab to a cozy Italian Restaurant on the Upper East Side.

It was known for being a celebrity hangout, and it didn't fail this evening. A famous couple that would remind you of us were there having dinner. As luck would have it, we sat across from them. The drinks started coming, and plenty of laughter filled my heart with love. "At Last," by Etta James, came on, and I felt that I had found a dream I could speak to. He was everything that I had dreamed of for myself. I knew the night was so special for no other reason except to celebrate our date. We looked into each other's eyes with so much passion and desire for each other. "I am really glad you came out with me tonight." "I am, too."

We both laughed and took a sip of wine. He had ordered a nice bottle of wine, and we drank that and then some. "Where should we go from here?"

I wanted him to decide for us, and he did so without hesitation. "Let's go across the street."

I looked out the window, and to my surprise, there was a line of people outside the building waiting to get into the concert to hear the Blues Travelers. A band that I had never heard of until that moment. He had planned this exactly how he wanted, and I enjoyed his company. "I'm ready to go when you are, sweetheart."

We both got up from the table and looked over at the couple next to us kissing each other. We grabbed hands and came together closely for the kiss of the night. He dipped me and kissed me at the same time. What a feeling of desire we had for each other at that moment! My thoughts were, "Forget the concert; let's go back to my place and make love all night." We headed across the street with a determination to get in without waiting in line. It just so happened that his good friend owned the place, and his name was on the list to get in, no question asked. We entered the club and found a perfect spot to hear the concert. "I'm so happy that you're here with me. I missed you these last few weeks while you were gone." He had a sincere look on his face that made it believable.

"I've missed you as well, Buttons."
"What do you want to drink?"

"I'll have vodka and soda with a lime twist." The bar was behind us and easy to get to for ordering. He walked over, ordered us a couple of shots and a drink, and then returned to our seats. "I thought we would have a shot to start off with, along with our drinks." He kissed me while handing me the drinks.

"A toast to a sexy lady whom I've missed."

The glasses touched with a clink, which was an indication that we could drink up. "I am happy to be back." Now, our relationship up to this point has been very simple: no questions asked, no strings attached. We had waited to jump into a sexual relationship for several months.

This night had all the makings of an extraordinary sexual experience. "Kiss me, you fool," mumbled Buttons. A kiss lasted way beyond what public affection should prohibit. "Kiss me even more than that, you fool." At this point, I felt the time had stood still with us.

Just then, the music started, and everyone began to scream. We looked at one another with uninhibited love. Feeling into the music only allowed us to feel more into each other. After several songs, we left for my place. The excitement of being with one another was there for us to explore. The mere fact that we couldn't keep our hands off one another was a sure indication of how connected we actually were to each other. Once we arrived at my place, we undressed each other with our minds. Our love began to develop into a magical feeling.

I knew that this could be the night we took our lovemaking to new heights. Passionately kissing one another, wrapped in each other's arms, felt like home. Our attraction towards one another was so powerful, with forces that felt like previous lifetime connections. Describing this feeling was an emotional desire, and how it made me feel at that moment was timeless. It wouldn't be wrong to say that our love was glorious; a timeless love best describes my feelings for him. I'll always love him.

One can always feel that love that warms your heart and makes you remember yesterday with the hope of new tomorrows. The fire between us ramped up each moment, allowing us to explore one another.

Chapter Eleven

Looking over at Brian, Grandma Kathrine knew he needed to eat dinner. "Let's have some dinner now while I finish up for the night."

He replied, "Absolutely, Grandma."

Dinner consisted of a Grilled Caesar salad with homemade dressing and another glass of wine. She could tell Brian was ready to hear her tell more of her story, so on with the show. She began with how the Baron was planning to travel with his family to celebrate his Birthday in New York City.

*****

The moments until we would meet again had weighed on me, and I was missing him madly, but today was the day the Baron would arrive in New York.

Shifting gears, I headed out to the Airport with our driver, eagerly anticipating his arrival so I could be there to greet him. He was traveling with his niece and nephew for his Birthday Celebration. Organizing a fun-filled week with everyone to help celebrate the joyous occasion was my priority for the week. This would be their first time in New York, so I wanted to exceed their expectations. I planned on showing everyone a grand time. I met them and their two young children, the first weekend I arrived in Belgium. We approached the airport right on time, and as I proceeded to the terminal where they would be arriving, a level of excitement came over me, knowing that the Baron would be back in New York City with me. Our love story had so many beautiful chapters up to this point, yet I knew we had just begun loving each other. The weather turned cold and felt like fall in New York. The last week of October meant Halloween treats and tricks filled the air in the city.

Interestingly, the Baron's Birthday was on Halloween, which was two days away. As the birthday got closer, I could feel my enthusiasm growing. Nevertheless, I made reservations for dinner at one of the best restaurants in NYC. This was sure to be his best celebration ever with his family. I could see them from a distance down the hallway from customs.

"Darling, is that you, my love?" He ran up to me and hugged my neck so tight that I could feel the love coming through his arms from his heart.

"It's me, darling." We stood there briefly, but it felt like we had never left one another's side.

"How was your flight?"

"It was short and sweet." The Baron turns to his nephew and niece, then introduces us again.

"Welcome to New York." I proceeded to walk over and hug them both. "Shall we head into the city?" As we headed for the car through the revolving doors, I thought of how magical this moment was for the baron, with his family by his side and showing them New York. A time of appreciation for just being with him. His true desire to show his family a memorable holiday was so precious, and it made me love him even more for being the kind of man I really wanted to be with every day.

This feeling was true love for me. As we arrived in the city, I could see the excitement on their faces at just seeing New York up close. It was overwhelming at first sight. Sophia, his niece, asked me, "How long have you been living in the city?"

My reply was simple: "Forever, it feels like. I've been living here off and on for the past eight years."

With a smile, "Do you love it here?"

"I do love it here. Every day is an adventure."

The Baron reached for my hand with such conviction towards loving me that my heart felt it. Pulling up to the hotel, I couldn't wait to get upstairs and make love to the Baron since it had been several weeks since we last loved each other. Arranging with his family when we would meet downstairs for dinner. All we could think of was making love to each other before dinner. "See you both at 8 o'clock for drinks before dinner. We have a car taking us to the Restaurant for dinner." Smiles sent us running upstairs and unlocking the door, throwing ourselves at each other and kissing each other passionately, two hearts becoming one in a heartbeat.

The passion between us awakened the soul from the darkness, where we no longer long for each other. The present moment was alive with love again. How we felt for one another at that moment was incredible.

"I love being with you, darling." He whispered.

"I've missed you, my love. I find it hard to be away from you."

After a long pause, he said, "You don't have to be away from me, darling. You can come live with me." All this after making love to one another.

It was a fabulous moment to talk about living with each other. My response was, "I would love to live with you." The Baron jumped up and poured the Champagne to make a toast. "Here is to our future together."

"I want to live here with you. Let's buy an apartment together here in New York City."

My eyes lit up with amazement at the idea of having a beautiful place in the city with him. "I want to start looking tomorrow with a Broker and find something before Christmas. Let's get ready and celebrate our news with my family."

I jumped up and started my bath, adding all the beautiful bath salts and bubbles to immerse my body in the pleasures of a bubble bath. I could feel the magic between us beginning to develop into a real bond. As I rushed to look and feel my best, I knew I had limited time to prepare for the evening, so I jumped into the clothes the Baron had purchased for me.

A selection fit for a Princess, along with shoes to match the outfit. The lifestyle was easy to accept and even easier to enjoy. "I'm ready, my love, for an evening full of fun with your family."

"Darling, you look so beautiful tonight. Let's go down and meet up with my family." I felt so much love between us at this moment, along with feelings of acceptance. This was a memory of a lifetime that I would never forget. As we arrived on the bottom floor, the elevator doors opened, and his niece and nephew were

seated in the lobby waiting for us to arrive. The evening had a magical feel to it. Everyone greeted each other with kisses from cheek to cheek. The Baron was on point to entertain his family and myself.

"Let's go have some fun, everyone." Upon our arrival, the restaurant greeted us with a fabulous table by the window with a city view. This Restaurant required a drive over the Brooklyn Bridge so you could look back at the reflection of New York City. A magical vision to see at night. A bottle of Champagne was being delivered as we sat down at the Hotel. "Here is a toast to my darling. Thank you for organizing this special evening with everyone." \The Baron stood and toasted this to me. "Avec pleasure, Moi Cheri," I replied. "I would like to let my family know that we plan to buy a place here in New York City and live between here and Belgium." They had a surprised look on their faces, to say the least, but they toasted us.

The news of us starting our journey together seemed so right at that moment that it bounced across the table straight to the waiter, who walked up with a grin on his face. "I can feel something special has brought you guys here tonight, so what's the occasion?"

"We are celebrating our future together with the world. When opportunity knocks at the door, open it and offer it Champagne."

That's just what we did at that moment. Everyone enjoyed the champagne and then moved on to the best dinner, which included their finest red wines and fresh seafood. After spending several hours with laughter and love, it was time to return to the Hotel. Our driver waited for us until we were ready to proceed. We made our way out to the car after thanking everyone who made the evening a huge success. Looking out at the city through the window, illuminating the entire car.

"What a spectacular view from here, my love." *Arriving at the Hotel, ready for a nightcap, we headed to the Bar for the last call.*

"Let's have an after-dinner nightcap before going upstairs, my love." *A round of drinks for all of us.*

"I'm always up for one more with you." *The romance between us felt so amazing that I couldn't wait to hold him upstairs. Once we finished up with the last call, it was upstairs for all of us. "Goodnight, everyone! Merci Beaucoup!"*

Once inside our room, I shouted, "At last, we are home!" This was all I could think of as we entered the room. Once the door shut, we heard the music playing in the room.

"It had to be YOU... Oh, darling, it had to be you." Singing away, he grabbed my hand and began to dance slowly to Ol' Blue Eyes. I felt so alive with each step in motion and each note of the song. It was an incredible moment. While he undressed me, I could feel the feelings of complete intimacy and wanted more of this in the bedroom. I took his hand and led him to the bedroom, where we began kissing each other passionately. His love was intoxicating to my soul, and the way he touched me made every inch of my skin tingle beyond explanation. All I could think about at this point was, Would this last forever? I knew that no matter what happened between us, I would enjoy the moments we created together. There's nothing sexier than a man who is in love with his woman and is not afraid to show it to the world, and this is exactly what the Baron did with me. I was overjoyed to be with Baron and wanted him to stay with me, like my soulmate, best friend, and the love of my life. His passionate lovemaking would send me into orbit, where I would experience ecstasy—an endless euphoria that had a special place in my heart. Time is so precious that I felt we were just stealing every bit of it. Together, *we could do anything, and I knew love conquers all.*

A birthday celebration was planned with the hotel Concierge for the Baron, and what an event we would make it! Starting with breakfast in bed, served with only a sexy smile. "Darling, it's your special day, and I want you to feel like a king." As he looked at me with so much love and desire, I embraced him with sexy kisses, then seduced him with my bedroom eyes.

This moment was ours to have and treasure forever. His love presented a new chapter in my life where the undiscovered dimensions met the reality of love. "A breakfast toast to the man I love on your big day." Breakfast mimosas, along with his favorite petite déjeuner, were on a beautiful silver tray on our bed. We fed each other down to the last bite, and the last sip was gone.

This meant it was time to shower and prepare for the day. His big day also happened to be Halloween, so the decorations in the hotel and around the city set the tone for the day. I had arranged with the Concierge for six tickets to Lincoln Center to watch Luciano Pavarotti in Puccini's "Tosca" and to follow it up with dinner at the Rainbow Room with everyone.

I had invited my friend Carol and her husband Charles to join us in celebrating his birthday. Dressed for the day, we proceeded to meet up with his family for lunch downstairs in the restaurant. As we waited for their arrival, thoughts of Buttons slipped into my memory, and his smile made love to me in my mind. His zest for life was singular. "Darling, is everything okay?" He asked me based on the look on my face.

"I am fine, darling; I am just feeling your love for me." This feeling would occur throughout the day and make me miss Buttons tremendously. I couldn't understand what happened to me, but I missed the warmth and comfort of Buttons. It felt like an eternity without him, and I couldn't wait until we reunited again.

Just in time to clear my mind, his family walked into the Restaurant. "Bonjour," the Baron greeted his nephew and niece. "Join us for a celebration of the day." The Baron began to explain his thoughts on how our new life together would transpire into reality. "We are so excited about purchasing our new Condo here in New York that we have hired someone to show us places today."

My face clearly expressed the story of the pure excitement of our love journey together. "How would you like to start looking at new homes today for us?"

At this point, lunch was finished in my book. Overwhelmed with the excitement of starting our life journey together, he had made our appointment with Blair, a top New York City real estate broker, to find our home in the sky. "Darling, I want to make you the happiest girl on the planet." My reaction was a huge smile from ear to ear.

"Would you guys like to join us?"

His nephew answered. "We want to take in the sights and sounds of the city. We will meet up with you both later in the afternoon."

Gathering our things from the table, the Baron answered, "Sounds like a wonderful game plan for the day. Enjoy." The doorman came over to us and announced our car had arrived, so away we went to explore the Real Estate market in New York City.

We had both agreed that the Upper East Side of Manhattan was our dream destination. Arriving at her office, the driver suggested we call him when we needed him to pick us up. "Give us a couple of hours; we are exploring the possibilities of buying a new home."

Without skipping a beat, he grinned and nodded at us. "No problem; I'll see you both later today. Let me know when you would like me to take you back to begin the Birthday celebration for you, sir."

The Baron replied. "Thank you for acknowledging my birthday. We have a spectacular day planned today, so off we go!"

"Good Luck."

As we walked into the building and approached the office, feelings of extreme happiness came over me, and without a doubt, I fell into them. We were starting our lives together in NYC, and it felt right. All the pieces were coming together so quickly, but the integrity was there, so that's why it felt right. A woman greeted us at the door and walked us into a conference room with big, bold leather chairs placed perfectly around the table. I pulled one out and sat down just enough to jump back up when Blair entered the room. "Hello, guys," with a bouncy attitude and smile to follow. "Are you ready to find your dream home?"

The feeling of love and compassion for one another could be felt in the room. We both turned and looked at each other with enormous grins. "Let's begin the journey on the Upper East Side."

"Ok," said Blair.

"We would like a place in the clouds. I know, let's call it our Condo in the Sky."

The Baron had a funny way of describing exactly what he wanted, but with his vision and Blair's insight, we would be ahead of the game. "I have mapped out the Upper East Side Condos for Sale at this moment. Anywhere between 5th Avenue and Park Avenue with breathtaking views to wrap yourself around.

"Shall we start with Park Avenue and work our way over to 5th? Can we have your driver take us around?"

Chapter Twelve

We called and told our driver the plan, and without hesitation, he was around the building waiting for us. We hopped in our car, and away we went to find our new home in the sky. "Please stop at 64th Street and Park Avenue; this will be our first stop. This Condo unit has a view of the park. Let's go see what you think about the views. Please wait for us here; we should only be about 15–20 minutes." Blair was affirmative with her direction.

"No problem," The driver replied.

The front door opened, and the doorman greeted us in French, which excited the Baron. With a smile on his face, the Baron replied, "Bonjour."

Blair asked for the keys to the unit on the 12th floor. The elevators were in the middle of the foyer, so we walked over to them, walked in, and took the ride up to possibly our new home. The elevator door opened on the 12th floor, and it just didn't feel like home. A small hallway gave the impression of having very low ceilings. Once we walked through the door into the unit, it just wasn't our dream home. "This is nice but not for us, and let's move on to the next one." The Baron knew what we wanted, and this wasn't it. "We would prefer a view of Central Park." Blair responded, "That is our next place on my list, so hang tight."

Whether it was or not, she was extremely smart to provide us with what we wanted. "The park would provide a sensational view for us to awaken every morning and celebrate our love with every sunset."

Blair answered, "Let's drive up to 84th Street and Madison Avenue." Traffic seemed heavy driving uptown, but the excitement in the car told another story.

"What a way to spend my birthday! I am in love with my soulmate and looking for our new dream place somewhere in the clouds where we can cherish each moment. I am the happiest man alive."

I kissed his hand and smiled at him with my heart. The driver pulled us up to the front of the building. "We have arrived at 84th Street." My first impression of the outside was that it was a very modern and relatively new building. We walked up to the front door, and the doormen opened the door with big smiles that invited us in.

"We are here to see 24B, please." Blair was exact with her words. They walked us over to the front

desk, where they would show us up and unlock the door for us. As the elevator opened on the 24th floor, there were two apartments, and B was to the right. The doorman opened the door, and nothing but views of Central Park awaited us. A spectacular feeling of just how magical New York City truly was could be seen inside this place. Without a doubt, this would be our home in the sky, or better, our Condo in the sky. You could see all the way to New Jersey on one side, and on the other side was all of Long Island. An unbelievable view! "What do you think of the place, darling?"

A quick response: "I LOVE THIS PLACE!"

The Baron turns to Blair with a firm voice and says, "This is our new home. We'll take it."

Blair's face lit up, and she smiled with excitement. "I will start the procedure right now. Please excuse me while I call my office."

The Baron took my hand and walked onto the balcony overlooking Manhattan. "You can see the GE Building to the Bronx Zoo; you can see everything in between."

"What a view, my love; I love it here. When can we start to decorate this place?"

The Baron jumped on it with, "Let's start tomorrow."

Blair looked at both of us and wanted an affirmative yes on the place. "Do you both love it?"

"Yes."

"Ok, then, let's start our engines and get this unit under contract. I know you both have a party to attend, so I will let you return to your hotel. I will let myself out after I've taken some photos for you both to review."

"Thank you for your time today and for showing us our new dream home."

We proceeded towards the door to catch the elevator. When the doors opened, we were greeted by the Doormen at the front desk. "What did you both think about the unit?"

"We loved it."

As we walked forward to our car, our driver was standing there waiting for us. "How did you like this one?" We both smiled at each other and then replied at the same time.

"We loved it, and this is our New Home in The Sky."

"Ready to head back to St. Regis now?"

"We are ready to start the celebration of one very important birthday and to find our beautiful new home." The driver replied, "Sounds like a big celebration is in order."

As he was pulling up to the Hotel, we invited him to take us out for our big night. "Will you be back here to pick us up in an hour?"

"No problem; I will be right here to pick you up whenever you are ready."

"Thank you." I dashed to the elevators and quickly showered before dressing in the finest dress the Baron had purchased for me, along with the beautiful jewelry.

I felt like a true Princess with a song in my heart. "You look so beautiful, my love."

I returned the compliment, "My love, you look so handsome."

A knock at the door sent us both rushing with anticipation. "Good evening and Happy Birthday, Uncle!" They had brought gifts with them. We walked into the sitting room, and a bottle of Champagne was ready for us to open when another knock at the door directed me in another direction. "Good evening, Carol and Charles; please join us in celebrating my true love's birthday."

They came to celebrate with us in style. We walked towards the celebration, where the Baron started preparing the Champagne flutes.

"Happy Birthday! We are so happy to be sharing this evening with you guys."

The wonderful sound of Champagne opening filled the room. Pop.

"Happy Birthday, Darling.' I kissed him with so much love and desire in my eyes.

"This is a wonderful evening to have family and friends helping my darling, and I celebrate my big day. Thank you for being here with me. Let us go and enjoy the show at Lincoln Center."

After opening a few gifts, we gathered our things and headed for the door. "The driver is waiting for us in a Limo, so there will be plenty of room." Everyone finished their glass of Champagne and proceeded to the door. Once downstairs, we followed each other to the car, where the driver greeted us with a smile. "Good evening, guys."

Everyone climbed inside, and off we went to Lincoln Center. The driver had a CD playing inside the Limousine of Pavarotti's greatest hits, including the songs we would hear at the performance. This music awakened the very core of romance within all of us, and once we arrived at Lincoln Center, the feeling of pure love for Opera and the lifestyle it represented hit me.

"Darling, I am forever grateful to you for creating the most amazing and memorable birthday ever."

The Baron smiled with such admiration.

"I love you, sweetheart." Once inside, we ordered a bottle of Champagne for those interested in having bubbles before the show. The night was magical for the mere reason we wanted to hear Luciano Pavarotti sing.

We had box seats for everyone, and we went to find them with our glasses of Champagne in hand.

"What an amazing view up here, darling. Thank you for organizing the best Birthday gift I've ever received."

"You deserve the best, darling."

Once the music started up from the Orchestra and the curtain went up, there stood Luciano Pavarotti playing the role of the painter Mario Cavaradossi in Tosca. A spectacular sight and an emotional feeling to hear his incredible voice, which would be a memory to treasure forever.

After the performance, we joined our driver for dinner at the Rainbow Room. The view from above Rockefeller Plaza on the 65th floor is breathtakingly stunning. A true New York institution with all its glamour and style. "Shall we go up?"

The moment we all gathered in the elevator, the experience transported us to another time. We stepped out of the elevator to a panoramic view of skyscrapers, historical prestige, and a woman waiting to greet us.

"Good evening, and welcome to the Rainbow Room. How many are in your party?"

"We're a party of six."

"Please follow me."

She walked us through a hallway with photos on either side of anyone and everyone. The best view from any window in Manhattan. We were about to experience the magic of the Rainbow Room. "Good evening," our waiter said, walking up and making the Baron's evening. "We are so thrilled you are dining with us on your Birthday."

The band was playing "I'm in a New York State of Mind," and I just wanted to dance with the Baron. "Darling, would you like to dance with me?"

"I thought you'd never ask."

Then, we were off to dance to a simply perfect song to set the mood. After a dip or two, we sat down with so much love in our hearts for one another. He whispered softly, "I love dancing with you, darling. I adore every step with you, Moi Cheri. Now, let's order a drink before dinner."

After the fabulous dinner, we had a special surprise for the birthday boy. "May I have your attention, please?" The singer from the band had everyone's attention.

"We have a very special birthday in the house. Please help me sing to our special guest." As everyone started to sing, the Baron stood up, grabbed my hand, and began to walk down to the dance floor.

The look on his face was priceless, and he joined in singing to himself. 'I love you, darling; this has been an extraordinary experience for a guy like myself. Thank you, my love."

All I could do was kiss him. "I love you, sweetheart. Let's go have some fun back at the Hotel."

"Let's go get crazy."

We returned to our seats when the band started to play Frank Sinatra's "You Make Me Feel So Young."

The Baron looked at me with those sparkling eyes and gratitude from his heart, which gave me so much love without words. I knew that he really appreciated the moment in time with all of us gathered together for his special birthday.

As we drove back to our hotel, everyone seemed in the best of spirits. "Thank you all for joining us this evening for a magical moment I will always treasure. I hope everyone enjoyed themselves as I did."

Everyone had a smile on their face that indicated all had a great time.

"Thank you, sweetheart, for a beautiful evening and for allowing us to participate in your celebration."

The Baron replied, "Avec plaisir."

Everyone slowly decided to go home or back to their room, which was the case for his niece and nephew. "Thank you for making this my best birthday celebration ever."

"Bon Nuit."

We decided to have our own celebration in the bedroom: "I have one more gift for you, my love, and it requires you to wait for it." As we were off to the bedroom, I changed into a very sexy outfit for the birthday boy's fantasy. "What do you think, my love?"

"I think I love you." He took my hand and began to kiss it until he reached my lips, where we kissed with a passionate force to take a risk into new territory. Lovemaking was so sexy between us, and wanting more was always my issue. I always wanted to chase him till dawn, and it's heartwarming that he wanted the same.

Chapter Thirteen

A bright, sunny day filled our room with music and the smells of fresh coffee from the other room awaiting us. I knew that the Baron would be returning to Belgium later today, so every minute counted.

"Rise and Shine to the smell of coffee."

"Good morning, Darling," I said after a long pause. "Bonjour, Darling, I don't want to leave you today; instead, I have decided to leave tomorrow and celebrate one more day with you. My family can return today without me. My flight has been changed already."

"That is fantastic news, darling. My heart was beginning to hurt knowing that you were leaving today. Let's make this the best day ever."

And that is what we did. Starting with petit-déjeuner, then morning sex before heading to the showers. Out the door and ready for the day, we went after quite a morning. A beautiful fall day with a cool breeze felt like Thanksgiving would soon be here. We were off to have lunch, with two Bloody Marys as our priority so we could plan the day. We walked across the street to a beautiful Sunday Brunch spot while walking to the sounds of a Tony Bennett song playing, "The way you look tonight," which made us both stop and hold each other for a moment while we kissed and sat down in the bar area.

The greatest music in the greatest city could only mean one thing: the drinks must be outstanding. One hit after another played while we ordered lunch and two Bloody Marys. "Darling, I am so happy that I decided to stay one more day. What would make you the happiest girl in the World today?" My first thought was going to a museum and taking in some culture, for he knew how to excite me with his knowledge of Fine Arts.

This would be a chance for us to bond and create a partnership for our upcoming life events. "Darling, what are you thinking?"

"I am thinking about us attending an exhibit at the Guggenheim Museum today. What would you think about doing something like that today?"

"I adore your appetite for educating yourself in the finer things in life. My job is to educate you with the knowledge I've obtained over my years of learning and studying the European Culture of the Fine Arts."

We finished our Bloody Mary's and paid our bill, then went off to the Guggenheim. The driver was waiting for us to make our next move from the car. He came around and opened the door for us to get out on the street side. "We will call you when we need your service. Thank you."

We stopped and stared at each other, then took a photo in front of the Guggenheim building, a photo that would last in my mind forever. We could capture the moment in time best with a photo, which held the feelings we shared for each other in that photo taken at that very moment in time. As we approached the doors of the Guggenheim Museum, I whispered in the Baron's ear, 'I love everything about you, my love."

He looked back at me and said, "IT HAD TO BE YOU, DARLING."

These were our words for each other. Time stood still once again for us, and without a doubt, love was our theme song. We entered the museum holding hands like school kids in love for the first time. Everything else faded away, and we were completely absorbed in the moment.

As we walked up the ramp to view the first exhibit, I saw a painting that caught my attention. "What a beautiful, inspired painting, my love."

The Baron turned to me with love in his heart. "I feel that is our love for each other, the way the lines curve and wrap around each other to give a warm hug."

I felt the same way.

"I am going to buy this painting for our new home together. This must be the centerpiece of our new place. When you walk into the place, this painting will be for all to view."

I completely loved this idea that we shared. The rest of the exhibit paled in comparison to the first piece we experienced. The Baron took down all the notes from the beautiful piece we loved and knew exactly what to do to purchase this piece of art.

"Do you love this piece like I do, darling?"

The answer came without a minute to spare, "Absolutely, my love, let's go celebrate our new baby with a glass of Champagne."

Later, we were off to celebrate once we located our driver, who was waiting for us outside. Once inside the car, our driver asked, "How was your time at the museum?" We both answered at the same time. "Fabulous!"

"Where shall I take you two love birds?"

"Back to the hotel, where we can have champagne in our favorite spot on the planet."

We sat at the bar and ordered a bottle of the finest Champagne and a bit of Caviar to go with the Champagne. "Let's satisfy our taste buds before heading upstairs to have sex before dinner."

It sounded like a perfect plan to me. After the last morsel of caviar was consumed and our last sip of Champagne, we headed upstairs to our room. Holding hands and kissing each other in the elevator stimulated our sexual desire for each other. The elevator doors opened, and as we entered our room, a beautiful arrangement of fresh-cut flowers had been delivered to our suite.

"Gorgeous flowers, darling. How do you think of everything?"

"My love for you inspires me to make all things beautiful in our world."

A setting for two with fresh glasses and poured Champagne, chocolate-covered strawberries, cheese, and crackers. Everything was arranged before we arrived. We sipped on the Champs, then went into the bedroom, where our kissing never ended. I slipped into the bathroom to put on sexy lingerie and powder my face while the Baron lit the candles in our room and set the mood for romance. "Darling, you look so sexy."

I snuggled into bed with love on my mind. "I love being with you, and I am so happy you decided to stay another day. What a day we've had, my love."

"One of our best days yet, and the best is yet to come, darling."

Kissing and loving each other was magical for us. As we celebrated our love for each other, a feeling of bliss came over me. I loved this man with every fiber of my being, and I could feel he loved me, too. The best way to describe our lovemaking for each other was sensational and romantic. "Darling, you make me feel like a young man. I want more of you every time we make love."

This was the ultimate compliment. "Let's have a bath together and prepare for dinner."

As he looked into my eyes, he whispered, "I will always love you, darling."

With that thought, I jumped up and started the bath with all the essentials needed to create a beautiful bubble bath. After enjoying the bath together, we proceeded to dress for dinner. He had made reservations at Le Cirque for 8 p.m. "Darling, I have a little something for you." I heard his voice whisper those words, so without hesitation, I walked into the other room.

"A little token of my love for you and our life together."

"My goodness, when did you step out and purchase this, my love?" A smile from ear to ear ran across his face.

I opened the beautiful box, and a pair of diamond earrings dazzled my eyes. "Wow! My love, what have you done, darling? These are amazing diamonds. Look at the sparkles."

"Do you love them?"

Without hesitation, I said, "I love them, darling, but not as much as I love you."

"Let's go have some fun, darling, and show off your ears. You do have the sexiest ears ever."

With that, I was off for an evening in NYC with a cheerful smile on my face and a kick in my step.

Our driver greeted us with a big hello from the front of the car. "Good evening, guys. Where is this beautiful fall evening?"

The Baron answered, "Off to Le Cirque at the Mayfair Hotel."

"A very good choice for dinner this evening."

We pulled up to the Hotel and entered the side door for dining at Le Cirque. The ambiance was electric, with a full light show and sexy seating for everyone to enjoy the elite people watching. A celebrity-filled room awaited us while we enjoyed each other. As we walked to our table, I noticed several familiar faces and thought of what their stories might be compared to mine. In a gigantic world, I felt like a precious being, somewhat like a princess, flaunting through time.

At this moment, I knew that our love together, composed of a single soul, was inhabited by two bodies. I had never felt so much love for a man, and I wanted this feeling to last forever. With all of these thoughts, at the same time, two Champagnes arrived, along with a big toast to each other.

"Darling, I had the best day of my life today, and if you would allow me to be your guy forever, every day could be this wonderful." I jumped up and kissed this man with every passionate fiber in my heart.

"I would be honored to spend all my days and nights with you, my love."

Toast!

The evening was about to get a whole lot sexier with those feelings. We had enjoyed a full experience together, from spending time with his family to celebrating his birthday to purchasing our Condo in the Sky.

"What is our next move, darling? When will we be together again?"

I didn't want to be sad about him leaving in the morning, so I barreled through the idea and came out on the other side.

"Let's think about where we want to spend the holidays together."

A toast for the holidays and for the upcoming experiences. Our waiter arrived to greet us and take our order for drinks and dinner. "May I interest you in a bottle of wine from our premier selection? We have the most exquisite wines from all over the planet and maybe one or two from Mars."

The Baron looked up with a chuckle and responded, "I want the bottle from Mars then." It was simply a joke to create a fun experience for all of us. "I think you should bring us the best Red Wine you have and two glasses."

"Yes, Monsieur, I will go get them while you decide on your dinner for tonight."

I could only imagine the bottle of wine about to be served to us. He knew exactly how to spoil me and what turned me on.

"Darling, what would you like for dinner tonight?" "I want you to order for me, sweetheart. Let's see what flavors you create for us this evening."

While he ordered for us, I recognized a very handsome man walking into the restaurant with a group of people. The very handsome man looked familiar to me, but I couldn't make out exactly who he was from a distance. As he walked closer to our table, it was very clear to me that my oldest boyfriend had just walked into the Restaurant. "Hello gorgeous, how are you guys this evening?"

Our connection was strong, and our love would always be there for each other. I wanted to kiss him, but without a shadow of a doubt, I knew to just stay quiet.

"We are doing fantastic, sweetheart. This is the Baron from Belgium and darling, and this is Jack from New York."

They both greeted each other and smiled back at me. This was an awkward moment, but one that would be revisited later. "Enjoy your evening."

We continued with our Champagne and kissed each other as I watched from the corner of my eye, Jack smiling back at me. Love will never be erased just because of time. "Darling, I have ordered our dinner and a delicious bottle of Red Wine." He continued without skipping a beat. I believed his curiosity could have gotten the best of him, but we had no time to waste, for this was our last night together for several weeks.

After celebrating our time together, we returned to our hotel for a nightcap. "Let's go visit our special bar of all bars."

Our driver found us walking out of the hotel and opened our doors for us to climb in and continue the celebration. "How was your dinner?"

"We love hanging out with the elite of New York and the World. Our dinner was delicious, as was the bottle of wine, not to mention the several Champagnes we had when we arrived."

He seemed happy to hear all about our evening. He stopped short of the hotel, and the Baron told him how much he appreciated him looking after us for the week. "Have a safe trip home, and I will be here when you return next time."

"I am planning on spending the holiday season here in New York, so I will have you pick me up from the airport in a few weeks."

'Sounds good."

We got out of the car and made our way to the bar just in time.

The corner table was open, so we sat down, and our favorite waiter came over to ask what we were drinking tonight. "We will have a glass of Champagne each." "Darling, I am so in love with you and want our new place to be amazing, like a cloud in the sky. Please start getting ideas for furniture, and I will wire the money into a joint bank account for us. Let's open that tomorrow morning before my flight. Would that be ok with you?"

I couldn't think of one reason why that would be a bad idea. "Of course, darling." He smiled at me and told me that he had arranged the meeting at the bank at around 9 a.m.

"I will be up with bells on and coffee in hand for the both of us."

We kissed one another passionately and began to make love with one thing in mind: Let's move this to the bedroom. "Darling, I have enjoyed this trip to New York with you, and I look forward to celebrating the holidays with you here in this magical city you call home."

There was more kissing between us, and finally, the lights went out, and the lovemaking between the sheets began.

"I love you, my darling."

Those were the last words I heard before sleeping.

Chapter Fourteen

The morning arrived with a hint of fall in the air. Reflecting upon the whole week spent in New York with the Baron, a wide grin spread across my face.

"Darling, your happiness is radiating across the room. What thoughts are dancing through your mind, my love?"

Balancing feelings of contentment and the impending departure, I simply smiled at him and whispered in his ear, "I love you."

Life is sweeter when infused with abundant love.

Knowing that his return to New York was just a few weeks away, bidding farewell was tempered by the anticipation of our next meeting. "Darling, let's make a quick trip to the bank and finalize the paperwork for our joint account."

After getting ready, we set out, stopping for coffee at a nearby cafe, the aroma of freshly brewed coffee enveloping us.

"Two coffees to go, please."

With the fragrant brew in hand, we proceeded to the bank. Walking a few blocks and entering the bank building, we were directed to a reserved area on the 21st floor for clients with substantial deposits. Enveloped in the grandeur of the surroundings, thoughts of how we would adorn our new Condo in the Sky began to take shape.

As we entered the elegant building, a genuine affection for the Baron filled my heart. Guided by the receptionist, we found ourselves in the office of Mr. Saul, a tall and handsome man who greeted us warmly. "Greetings, I'm Mr. Saul, and I'll be assisting you today. What are your intentions for the joint account you wish to open?"

The Baron's response was swift and purposeful. "We intend to establish a joint account to create a haven in the sky where we can draw funds to decorate and maintain our new Condo."

Mr. Saul assured us of the account setup and began the paperwork. Amidst the process, the Baron and I exchanged a knowing glance, feeling the connection deepen.

Our signatures sealed the deal, and as we bid Mr. Saul farewell, anticipation mingled with the certainty of our shared future. "We did it, my love. Our joint bank account to bring our Condo dreams to life."

A tender kiss punctuated our joyous achievement. Reluctantly, the Baron had to depart for the airport, but with the assurance that he would return in a few weeks. "Goodbye, for now, my love. Until we meet again."

***

As the Baron left, Grandma Kathrine returned to reality, where her grandson Brian and she resumed their conversation, his understanding of her life's journey deepening.

"Grandmother, what a captivating chapter of your life. The Baron truly showered you with unforgettable moments."

She nodded, appreciating his empathy and insight. With the evening advancing, she suggested it was time to sleep, and Brian agreed, carrying the enchanting narrative to his dreams.

The next morning found them at the familiar spot, gazing at the sunrise in unison, a testament to life's magical unfolding. Maria served them a hearty breakfast, her warm presence adding to the moment's serenity.

"A cup of coffee, Brian?" Maria's offer was met with gratitude as they enjoyed the breathtaking hues of the morning sky.

A deep sense of satisfaction filled Grandma Kathrine as she observed the ocean, a testament to the happiness her life had been blessed with.

Brian's inquisitive gaze met hers, prompting his question, "How are you feeling today?"

She responded honestly, "I'm feeling better after my coffee. Another doctor's appointment awaits next week, and I'm hopeful for answers."

Brian's unwavering support had renewed her determination to face whatever lies ahead.

With plans for the day ahead, she asked Brian, "What shall we do today?"

His unexpected decision to extend his stay and continue delving into her story for his project was met with genuine delight. As they contemplated the intertwined paths of love and destiny, Brian's decision to remain by her side felt like a gift.

She replied without hesitation. "I would be honored to have you for the weekend. Let's conclude my narrative so you can craft your own for your school project."

Brian readily agreed, recognizing that delving into the entire story would aid his assignment.

***

At that juncture, my emotions for the Baron surged with remarkable intensity, and the knowledge of our impending reunion in just a few brief weeks added to my sense of anticipation. This anticipation, in turn, set the stage for our shared preparations leading up to Thanksgiving.

My dear friends, Carol and Charles, warmly requested our presence to partake in their Thanksgiving celebration at their inviting apartment. The ambiance promised to be delightful, adorned with Carol's culinary prowess and Charles's hearty appetite. The table would groan under the weight of delectable homemade dishes. While fleeting moments of longing for Buttons, my faithful companion, would sometimes surface, the vibrant calendar that the Baron and I shared left little room for such sentiments. My heart was determined to savor each fleeting moment with him. As for the future, I knew it held the promise of renewed intersections, albeit at a later date.

Time passed swiftly, and before I realized it, I found myself headed to the airport, eager to welcome the Baron for the week preceding Thanksgiving. Our schedule was brimming with a delightful array of activities leading up to our shared holiday celebration. It marked his inaugural Thanksgiving experience in the States, and I was determined to make it an unforgettable time in the vibrant city of New York.

As the airport appeared during the journey, I noticed a message notification on my phone. It was from Blair, extending a gracious invitation to a dinner party in our honor. The message read...

"Please allow me to host a New York dinner party for you and the baron on Saturday night at our home on Park Ave."

I eagerly replied, "We would be absolutely delighted to accept your invitation for tomorrow night." Motioning for my driver to wait, I quickly headed inside to welcome the Baron and assist with his luggage. Our eyes met, and with genuine affection, he exclaimed, "Hello, my darling. The joy of being back in your embrace is beyond words." We shared a passionate kiss that seemed to stretch indefinitely, momentarily forgetting about his circling baggage, which caught our attention.

Amidst the excitement, a text notification illuminated my phone screen. It was the news that we had been invited to Blair's residence the following evening, a gesture to celebrate our relationship and our new shared abode among the clouds. I responded promptly, confirming our enthusiastic acceptance and assuring the Baron that he needn't worry about my response. "Yes, my love, we would be absolutely thrilled to attend. I've missed you immensely during our time apart. I can hardly handle my happiness now that we're together again."

We stepped out to the curbside, where the Baron's luggage was efficiently loaded into the awaiting Town car. Settling in, we embarked on the drive back to the city, arriving at the grand entrance of the St. Regis Hotel, where the welcoming doorman awaited. Our entrance was seamless, and after a swift check-in, we found ourselves in the suite, greeted by a pleasant surprise. A bottle of Champagne awaited us, along with a thoughtful note that read...

"Welcome back to New York. We are happy to see you both and hope you have a fabulous stay with us."

"Now that is exceptional service," remarked the Baron with a grin. He uncorked the bottle and poured us each a flute of Champagne. A delicate spread of caviar and its accompaniments awaited us—a true display of top-tier hospitality. "Truly first-class treatment," I acknowledged. We indulged in the exquisite offerings and found ourselves entwined in a passionate embrace.

"My longing for you, my darling, is immeasurable. I feel incomplete without you," I

confessed, a smile conveying the depth of my affection and admiration. "The time we spent apart felt far too lengthy, and I yearn for your presence each day." Determination to bridge the gap began to take shape in my thoughts, although I chose to let the current moment bask in our intimacy. Soft kisses lingered, preserving the intimacy that had just transpired.

After dressing, we descended to our favored bar. "Where should we dine tonight?" became the subject of our discussion. A mutual decision led us to the esteemed Caviar House, a haven of epicurean delights. "I'll settle the bill, and we can arrange for the driver to take us," I suggested, eager to extend the evening's pleasures.

All I could think of was more Champagne and Caviar. Upon entering the splendid ambiance of the Caviar House, a symphony of flavors awakened my senses. It was an irresistible invitation and one that we gladly accepted. Decision-making became a delightful task, the array of choices evoking anticipation for an evening of culinary indulgence. As we savored the delectable offerings, the prospect of a passionate encore awaited us beneath the sheets.

"Good evening to both of you. I am Ana, and I will be attending to all your needs and desires this evening.

What can I get you both to start with in terms of cocktails?"

Ana, a statuesque brunette with Eastern European features, stood before us. While I intended to inquire about her background later, my immediate focus was on the Champagne.

The Baron responded in French, exuding a charming and alluring accent. "We will begin with a bottle of your finest Champagne to set the tone for this captivating evening."

The ambiance was in play, with all the characters ready to enjoy the evening. "Darling, let's order caviar for three and invite Ana to join us in sampling each variety,"

I appreciated the sentiment guiding his intentions. As Ana returned with our Champagne bottle, her actions further emboldened me. She arrived bearing three Champagne flutes, prompting, "May I partake in a toast to my new friends?"

We welcomed the addition of a newfound friend in New York with enthusiasm. As the Champagne was poured into our flutes, palpable positive energy enveloped us. The convergence of our backgrounds and the suspended sense of time made this moment truly special.

"Darling, let's order the finest caviar for all of us to experience. Two containers of your best and the fixings to go along with them. How long have you lived in New York?" The Baron asked Ana.

"I have been here for two years. I am from Budapest." She lit up when speaking about her Country. The Hungarian people are enriched by their culture and country.

"Have you been to Budapest?" She asked us.

"I have not been to Budapest, but I would love to visit your Country one day."

The caviar was elegantly presented on a silver platter, enough to bring a smile to anyone's face. The array of colors on the dish delighted our senses. The time had come for us to partake in the caviar feast.

"Ana, would you care to join us for some caviar?" I asked.

The atmosphere between us was serene. Ana politely excused herself to assist her other patrons, promising to return. We were unexpectedly enveloped in an atmosphere of seduction, aligning with my desire to share such experiences with the Baron.

Sometimes, life's most unforgettable moments occur spontaneously; one simply needs to be receptive to the opportunity. After attending to her other table, Ana eventually joined us, and we raised our glasses in another toast. "Here is to our evening together."

As our eyes connected with each other, a sensual moment began for us. Sharing our feelings for each other felt free to explore. There were no boundaries to hold us back. We finished our dinner and called for our driver. "Let's head over to the Monkey Bar," I suggested. It was a perfect spot to unwind, listen to some live music, and enjoy the evening. We hopped into the car, and our driver navigated through the bustling New York streets.

As we arrived at the Monkey Bar, the familiar tune of jazz melodies greeted us.

"The more you drink, the better I sound," the singer announced between songs, drawing chuckles from the audience. We found two seats at the bar, and the bartender promptly brought us two glasses of Champagne and two glasses of water, a balanced choice for the night.

With each soulful note that the singer crooned, our eyes met, and an unspoken understanding passed between us. It was moments like these that made our connection even stronger.

"I love you, darling," he whispered, his words dancing in the air. Time seemed to pause, allowing us to relish the enchanting ambiance of the bar and the warmth of each other's company.

"Thank you, Michael, for another fabulous evening," I called out to the singer before we said Goodnight and headed over to the St. Regis Bar. He smiled at us, and I blew him a kiss on the way out. "It's always a fun evening listening to Michael sing the songs we grew up enjoying."

The night air was crisp, and our driver was ready to take us back to the St. Regis Hotel. Drinking Champagne in New York City with my sweet Baron and looking forward to spending time with him was the top priority. Our hearts were light, and our spirits were high, knowing that the best was yet to come.

"We're returning to the hotel now," I informed our driver as we settled into the back seat.

"How was your evening?" he inquired with a friendly smile.

"We had a wonderful time at the Monkey Bar, and the night is still young," I replied with a mischievous grin.

As we approached the hotel, a serendipitous sight caught our attention. A street artist was creating a vibrant mural on a nearby wall.

"Let's stop for a moment and admire this artwork," the Baron suggested. We stepped out of the car and stood in awe as we watched the artist's skilled hands bring the canvas to life. As we walked toward the elevator, I asked the Baron, "How was the evening, darling?"

"We have had one sexy evening, and the best is yet to come.' This was very encouraging for me. It felt like a dream.

We made our way up to our suite with sex on our lips and love in our hearts. The romantic evening that we shared was like making love to the city. We knew the passion between us was real when we kissed each other. Our connection deepened as our lips met, affirming the authenticity of the fervor between us. Upon opening the door, a shared gaze ignited a magnetic pull, drawing us together in a passionate kiss. We had no idea that the Champagne bottle had already arrived before us. How was that possible? Kissing in the elevator might have allowed the bartender to advance in front of us.

"May I pour you a glass, my love?"

That was probably going to be the last for the evening.

"I would love to join you in a nightcap, darling." The music in the room was that of Pavarotti, and it made for a romantic setting. The mood was set, and the lovemaking began with that first kiss.

Chapter Fifteen

The atmosphere was electric, and the Baron's eyes sparkled with anticipation. As our lips met in a passionate kiss, I felt a surge of excitement pass between us. Without breaking our gaze, I gestured for him to join me on the sofa. Eagerly, he moved closer, his desire palpable.

Our connection had grown intense over our conversations, and he knew I was relishing this moment. For me, the simple act of touching his skin was a thrill in itself. The chemistry between us was undeniable, and it was clear that the Baron was just as captivated.

As our hands explored each other's bodies, a sense of comfort and intimacy enveloped us. We decided to take things further and move our escapade into the bedroom. Stripping off our clothes and leaving them behind in the parlor, we embarked on a journey of shared pleasure. His lips met mine, and I could feel the heat of his desire. In a daring move, he kissed me again fervently while his hands caressed my skin, sending shivers down my spine.

"What an amazing experience!" I thought to myself. The stimulation turned faster with the tempting erotica that made the two of us fully immersed in sexual fulfillment.

"Wow," was the first word that came out of the Baron's mouth. "I have never experienced such pleasure with a beautiful and very sexy woman. This is one of the best nights of my life!"

What could you possibly add to that statement?

"I am so happy that you feel that way, sweetheart," I responded with a smile.

His eyes met mine, and he just stared hard, like all my secrets were right there on my face. I ran my hands over his hair. His fingers trailed over my shoulder and stopped at my collarbone just before they reached my neck. We kissed each other passionately. We adjusted ourselves until we were facing each other, sharing a pillow. "Good night, darling," the Baron said to me. "Good night, my love," I leaned forward and kissed him. I kept staring at him for a few moments and then went to sleep.

As the sunlight woke me up early, I got up and ordered a continental breakfast for two. The night had left me with a satisfying hunger, and my cravings extended to a strong cup of coffee. With the convenience of an in-room espresso machine, I helped myself to a cup of coffee, awaiting the arrival of the complete pot.

The breakfast was brought to our room, and with its arrival, the Baron woke up. His alluring voice greeted me with, "Good morning, darling."

With a smile gracing my lips, I replied, "Good morning, my love. I've got everything ready to kick-start our day."

He expressed his satisfaction, saying, "Excellent."

As we had our breakfast, we delved into planning the day ahead. "We should get a little something as a gift for Blair's dinner soiree at her Park Avenue residence," the Baron suggested. "And I would love to take a leisurely stroll with you through Central Park. It's a splendid fall day – perfect for some outdoor activity. How about lunch at the Boathouse?"

I agreed, "Sounds like a wonderful plan. Give me an hour to organize everything, and we'll be set."

I made a call to the Concierge to ensure our transportation was ready for the evening's soiree. "Could you please arrange for our favorite driver to pick us up around 6:45 pm? Thank you." With that task underway, I turned my attention to the next item on the list – finding a suitable gift. With Tiffany's conveniently en route to the park, it seemed like the ideal place to search for a token of appreciation.

I swiftly stepped into the shower, and within the hour, we were ready to leave, heading towards Tiffany's. In a swift yet stylish manner, I dressed for the day, coordinating my outfit with a matching bag and shoes. One of the highlights of New York City was its charm during Thanksgiving time, adorned with enchanting decorations in windows and adorning the streetlights. The holiday spirit enveloped the entire city.

Entering Tiffany's, we were greeted by the captivating sight of diamond rings and earrings displayed in the first showcase, radiating an exquisite allure. "Darling, I'll catch up with you on the upper floor while you explore the home department for a gift. I'll see you shortly," he said.

I took the elevator up to the home department, where I thought something for a bottle of wine to be poured from or placed on would be an appropriate gift.

I knew that wine would be served at Blair's dinner, and as she had inquired about the Baron's wine preferences, I initially considered wine goblets.

However, I ultimately settled on a silver wine holder, which I thought would make the ideal gift. Just as I concluded my purchase and turned around, I found the Baron at the register with me. "Hi, Darling."

I answered, "I found the perfect gift for Blair and her husband."

"Then let us be on our way," he replied.

We walked across the street and again to place ourselves in front of Central Park. I knew it would take us a good 30 minutes to reach the boathouse, and by that time, we would have worked up an appetite for lunch.

It never failed to amaze me how spectacular Central Park was in the Fall time. The vibrant shift in leaf colors turned the park into a captivating haven of natural beauty, a picturesque panorama that always took my breath away.

The cool air was buzzing through my hair, and there was a chill just enough to put a kick in step. It took us no time to reach our destination. A table strategically positioned to overlook the small lake that gracefully curved around the park. The Baron confidently approached the hostess, his words elegantly requesting, "Good day, we would like the best seat in the place, please. A view would be splendid."

Though in truth, there wasn't a single seat that didn't offer a wonderful vista. With a gracious smile, the hostess replied, "Certainly, please follow me."

We settled into our seats beside the tranquil lake, its surface close enough that we could almost reach out and touch the water. "Darling, is this perfection at its finest?"

"Absolutely," I nodded.

The waitress arrived to take our order for cocktails. "Hello, we will have two glasses of Champagne, please," the Baron requested.

The weather was truly exceptional, a fitting backdrop for our leisurely park stroll and lunch at the Boathouse. I quickly glanced at the menu and decided on a salad. "Our time together is priceless, and the memories we are creating have touched my heart and soul."

A sudden intensity filled the Baron's gaze as he leaned in to kiss me, a kiss infused with the passion of a once-in-a-lifetime love. "Seems like one of those postcard-worthy moments, my love," he remarked. The concept of "postcard moments" was something we often cherished – those instances worthy of preserving on a postcard and tucked away in a scrapbook.

They were days destined to become cherished memories, the kind you'd look back on as the golden days of life.

As we enjoyed our lunch along the water, I received a phone call from the Hotel reminding me that our car would be ready at 6:45 pm to take us to Blair's place for our dinner soirée.

"We are all set for tonight, darling," I remarked, exchanging a smile with the Baron before returning to our lunch. "Darling, we have time to sneak up to the Metropolitan Museum if you feel like a little culture." Without skipping a beat, he replied, "Absolutely."

The walk up to the Museum was about 10 minutes from where we were having our lunch, so we hurried up and paid our tab to take in the culture of New York City. This museum housed all the great Impressionists from the origins of Impressionism.

Among the pieces that caught the Baron's attention were those by Gustave Courbet, which he planned to adorn our new condo with. I couldn't wait to see some of Gustave Courbet's work in The Metropolitan Museum and get a feeling of where to place it in the Condo. Climbing the steps to the museum's entrance, it struck me just how close our new residence would be to this hub of culture. The thought of enjoying our morning coffee at the small tables outside the museum before indulging in artistic treasures became all the more appealing. Once inside the museum's walls, we checked our coats and bags, secured our tickets, and ascended the initial flight to the first tier of stairs.

I could tell that this excited the Baron. He had an immense passion for the arts and would often share his knowledge about significant works that held personal meaning for him. "Darling, when you return to Belgium, I simply must take you to The Maison du Roi, the King's House. You will find items from our family's Estates Collection that have been donated," he explained, revealing a glimpse into the treasures his family held. I could only imagine the magnificence of the collection that once graced his family's homes, and I was aware of the significance they held, particularly considering the tumultuous history during the Nazi era. They recovered most of them because his father worked for them every day. What a life that must have been for them, knowing that on any given day, they might never see their father again. "Darling, let's begin to feel into the masterpieces. They truly are a step back in time," he suggested. It was a magical feeling to actually allow yourself to go back in time and see the works of Art these amazing artists created. I agreed, finding it almost enchanting to step into history and witness the artistic creations of these exceptional talents.

We toured each section with amazement for the talent each piece looked like hanging up in the Met. "Darling, here is our guy Gustave Courbet. I am having three of his paintings shipped to our new Condo in the sky."

My head had a hard time wondering what that would look like in a Condo, but I was thrilled at the opportunity.

The enchanting masterpieces ignited a deep sexual excitement, and I found myself leaning over to kiss the Baron. He playfully responded, "Perhaps we should sneak away for a little rendezvous before the soirée tonight."

With a lingering look at the captivating room filled with timeless art, I agreed, saying, "Let's go, Darling.'

Exiting the museum, we descended the steps and hailed a cab to return to our hotel. In the spacious taxi, our hands couldn't resist each other, and our passion was palpable. Upon arriving back at our room, we wasted no time undressing each other and engaging in a passionate lovemaking session akin to an artist meticulously painting a masterpiece.

"Darling, I want to spend the rest of my life with you." The sincerity of my words reflected the profound love I held for him, this extraordinary man who had become my world. His reply was equally heartfelt, "I would love to spend the rest of my life with you, as well." With an intense gaze, we resumed our passionate kisses, losing track of time until I glanced at the clock. The realization that we were due downstairs in an hour jolted me into action, and I quickly got up and headed for the shower, promising, "I'll join you shortly. I love you, sweetheart."

Our love story would be told to the world one day, and I would want the world to know how much he meant to me. All I could think of now was being on time for the dinner soirée in our honor. I took each step in preparing for a fabulous evening with the love of my life.

***

Turning her attention back to Brian, Grandma Kathrine couldn't help but notice the hunger. He needed something to eat – whether it was breakfast, brunch, or even lunch. She decided it was time to take care of his appetite.

"Let's have Maria whip us up a meal. This story is making me hungry, and I can only imagine how famished you must be," she suggested, a smile forming on her lips. He returned the smile, his expression confirming his hunger. "Maria, could you prepare a hearty breakfast for two? Surprise us," Grandma Kathrine requested, and she chuckled before heading to the kitchen. It was amusing to her to think of them as a Baron and Baroness. She and Brian settled back, ready for a satisfying meal to come their way.

Taking a moment to shift the focus, she turned to Brian. "How about sharing some stories from your childhood? We've been delving into my past, but I'm eager to hear about your early days." Brian glanced her way and began to recount his upbringing in New York City. "My parents provided me with a remarkable education that led me to an Ivy League college. Their love made my childhood wonderful, and my father often spoke of my grandmother as his role model. She was a strong and influential presence in his life," he shared. "I really wish that you and I could have spent more time when I was growing up in New York, but I know now that you were traveling the world with all your many causes," he added.

He spoke fondly of Grandma Kathrine, who had left a lasting impact on everyone. Brian continued saying that he truly felt grateful to be able to hear these stories and to learn more about his family history, and he felt inspired by the example of his grandmother's strength, resilience, and compassion. At the same time, she felt a twinge of regret for not being as present during his formative years as she thought to herself.

"I kept the postcards you sent me while I was growing up. They meant a lot, especially during the times I felt your absence," he revealed.

Feeling determined to bridge any gaps, she encouraged him, "We have much catching up to do, so let's move forward together."

Just as she finished speaking, Maria approached them with a hot plate of breakfast – eggs, bacon, and toast. "Gracias, Maria," they expressed their gratitude.

The delicious breakfast provided the nourishment they needed as they delved back into their tales. "Please, continue with your stories after you finish that bite of breakfast, of course," said Brian.

"I'll continue from where we left off, my dear Grandson," she was ready to resume their storytelling. She turned to Brian, inquiring, "Remind me, where did we leave off?" Brian promptly responded, "You were in the process of getting dressed for the grand dinner soirée."

Chapter Sixteen

The time had arrived for us to meet up with our driver. "Darling, will you come in here quickly so we can have a quick glass of Champagne?"

"You look so handsome, my love." His smile met me at the door. "I have something beautiful that I saw today and couldn't resist."

"What have you done, darling?"

"First, give me one small kiss, and I will present them to you." What in the world was the thought playing in my head?

One very passionate kiss and one small blue Tiffany's box appeared from his coat pocket.

"What?"

"To the most sparkly woman I have ever met, I want you to always shine."

As I opened up the box, the most beautiful diamond ring magically appeared.

"Stunning, darling, when did you have time to sneak this into your bag?"

"Remember when I told you to run along and buy Blair's gift for the party? I found this quickly and had

the girl wrap it and place it in the little blue Tiffany's bag. What do you think of them?"

I replied, "Let me put them on now. They are stunning, my love."

They were beloved and timeless accessories with a touch of charm. I went up to the mirror while the Baron poured us a glass of Champagne. Remember this moment, I told myself.

"Here is to our love, darling. You are the one that I want to spend the rest of my life with and travel the world with, darling."

I couldn't hold back the tears, so I wiped my eyes so I wouldn't ruin my makeup. "You sure know how to make a girl smile."

We drank our Champagne, and off to the party we went, with a gift in hand. I picked up the other Tiffany bag, the one I purchased, to avoid confusing it with the one my beautiful earrings came in. Then, we went off to meet up with our driver. Right on time, may I add, and not a minute to spare?

"Where am I taking you cats tonight?" Asked our driver.

"We are headed to Park and 64th Street, please." The ride took us only 10 minutes, and once at the

location, he opened our car door, and we walked up to the doorman. "We will call you when we are finished."

He answered back, "No problem."

The doorman told us which floor to go to and walked us to the elevator, where another man took us up to Blair's apartment. We rang the bell, and a woman dressed in a beautiful dress opened the door and greeted us. "May I take your coats and any other items you wish to leave with me?"

The Baron helped me out of my coat, and I carried my small clutch, along with the blue Tiffany's bag, into the main room.

"Hello, Blair." Everyone turned and looked at us when we entered the room.

"Hello, everyone! I want to introduce my newest friends and clients. This is Kathrine and the Baron."

We smiled at the few people in the room.

She had her husband, Frank, and their two grown children with their spouses and a few friends. This was going to make for an interesting evening.

"May I get you something to drink?" Asked the lady who took our coats.

"Champagne, please"

"Yes, and for you, sir?"

"I will have the same as my darling."

Blair's home was decorated with art from around the Globe. I could tell she was well-traveled from the pieces of Art and paintings she had acquired on the wall. After spending the day at the Museum, my eyes were a bit refined in the arts, shall we say?

"Let's make our way to the dinner table, everyone. I have seating arrangements for everyone to step out and meet a new friend."

My seat was next to her husband, Frank, and the Baron was seated next to Blair. Imagine that one. I could tell that she was fascinated by him. "May I pull in your chair for you, Madame?" I looked up, and Frank was saying this to me. "But of course, you may, sweet Frank."

We began to chat it up with one another when the first course arrived.

Caviar and cream on a beautiful plate, delicious elegance on a small plate.

I looked over at the Baron, and he was winking back at me. This made me feel sexy.

"Please, may I have your attention, please?" Blair stood up and made a toast on our behalf. "I want to thank my guest for coming and look forward to a

delightful evening with family and friends."

She also had a gift for us, so I handed her our gift as well.

"Let's open our gifts together. You go first, Katherine."

I stood up and opened this very large blue box from Tiffany's. Wrapped so precisely with silver wrapping paper, along with a white ribbon surrounding the package.

As I opened the box along with the Baron, we both loved them at first sight.

"These are beautiful Champagne flutes. Wow, Thank you, Blair."

She smiled at me. "Now it is your turn, Blair."

Another blue Tiffany's bag. Great minds think alike. Everyone sat around the well-decorated table, with lavish China and a silver runner draped over the antique table. I admired the gift while she was opening it in front of us.

"Thank you so much for this beautiful silver wine holder. I will place it on our table this evening as we drink to our new friendships."

A delicious red wine was being served with dinner and champagne for anyone who desired that over red wine. I just so happened to be that one at the table. The waiter came around, asking if I would care for another glass of champagne. "May I serve you another pour?"

"Yes, please," was my response.

The light jazz music could be heard ever so lightly throughout the apartment, which made for a rich cultural mood. Soft music resonates with our emotions and spirits perfectly.

Our lawyer and his wife joined us, so there were more than enough to call it a dinner party. Blair had prepared a four-course dinner for everyone, and that was exactly what we all enjoyed. The time flew by, and it was a magnificent evening.

"Thank you all for making this evening so special. We look forward to many more occasions where we can celebrate young love and old love with everyone here. Until we meet again, Goodnight."

As we got up and retrieved our Tiffany box, the young lady came up to me and handed me my coat. "Merci."

A big hug to Blair and her husband, along with their kids. A spectacular moment for us, and now we were headed back to the hotel, where we would have a nightcap in the bar.

The driver was waiting for us downstairs and jumped out as soon as he saw us. "How was your evening?"

I spoke up while getting inside the car. "A fabulous dinner party for us. A true celebration of our love as a couple."

*We kissed one another while riding over to our hotel. "Darling, our story is a true romance with all the elements to be a successful movie. I think the title should be **"A LITTLE LUCK and a LOT OF LOVE."** He smiled and kissed me.*

"I know for myself that this is a fairy tale that I could only dream of as a little girl. I wouldn't change a thing about what we've shared together or all our plans for the future together. The way we met, the way we kissed and made love, and the way you love me, I am a very happy girl."

"You are home for the week. Home away from home, or should I say until your home is finished and furnished with the most beautiful furniture?"

That would remind me of my shopping tomorrow with an interior decorator at the furniture market. "I will be up early to check on some pieces I am looking to furnish our new home in the sky." The Baron smiled at me, stepped out of the car, and walked up to the driver with a tip. I headed inside the hotel, where I would check on our tickets for tomorrow night's performance with Frank Sinatra.

This would be a postcard moment, along with an early dinner at Cipriani's. A perfect way to prepare your Italian vibe with the best Italian food and Frank. I had it as a surprise for the Baron, so I signaled to him that I would meet him in the bar.

"Good evening, Kathrine. I have your itinerary for tomorrow's events, and all your lunch and dinner reservations have also been made. It sounds like a fun-filled day for both of you."

"Thank you very much for all your help with these plans. I will pick everything up tomorrow morning on my way to breakfast."

"That will be fine. Goodnight."

I headed for the bar to see my love waiting for me with a glass of bubbles.

"A stool awaits you, darling."

I could hear him speaking from a distance, with a lot of sexy tunes in his voice.

"I am right here, my love." I jumped up on the bar stool and began to pick up my champagne flute when the Baron raised his glass first to toast us.

"To the one true love of my life. May your love for me always remind you of tonight."

As the glasses touched, a vibration was felt from them, which sent a smile to both of our faces. "This is a perfect night, with the perfect mate and a perfect moment shared by all." Another sip of champagne, and up to the room. We enjoyed this amazing day and night with all its beauty.

"Thank you so much for my new piece of jewelry. I love my new earrings from Tiffany's."

Kiss to seal the love for all he meant to me at that moment. I was off to bed after one long day of getting it done.

A storm had rolled into Manhattan overnight, leaving the city with a blanket of snow, so awakening to a winter wonderland in November was a very sexy feeling. I stepped into the living room, where I could open the curtains, wrap up in a blanket on the sofa, and stare out at the beautiful view of the snow. A small breakfast item, such as juice, coffee with fresh cream, a couple of croissants, and a small bowl of berries, was ordered with room service.

I turned on the jazz radio in the room, sat quietly, and meditated. I was appreciating all that was coming my way in life. It is a lifetime of love and memories to tell future generations what it means to love someone. The doorbell rang, and they let themselves in with an elegant table full of morning treats.

"Good morning."

I responded. "Good morning," right back to him. The coffee woke me up without even having a sip.

"You can just leave it there in the middle of the room."

As I signed the ticket, the Baron walked in to join me. "Bonjour." We all smiled at each other. Petit Déjeuner was his favorite meal of the day, and it was mine as well. He sat beside me on the sofa and described his amazing journey through life. He began to tell me how growing up in Belgium was for him during those unbelievable times. "Darling, as the history books have noted, the German military was a brutal tribe of beasts, and how they made our family suffer will never be forgotten. Please promise me you will continue to tell this story even after I am gone. I have only you to tell this story to, my love. When we have a child or two, if God wants, they can carry on the family name and the traditions."

My eyes grew with amazement at this kind of news. I really enjoyed where this was going, but I had no idea that those were his feelings toward having a family together. He knew how important having a family was to me, and starting a dialogue with me hopefully meant that we would start focusing our attention on building a family. We had big plans for today. Breakfast of Champions downstairs in the main dining room and an early dinner at Cipriani's, then off to see Frankie.

"One hell of a day we will have together!"

Then, I was off to the bathtub to pick out the perfect outfit for the day while keeping the evening wear separate.

"I will be right back, my love." He stood up to give me a kiss and poured himself another cup of happiness. The coffee sends you into a euphoric state of mind and keeps you there all day. After getting dressed, we were ready for breakfast at the hotel. I could only think of lunch later, but I knew I needed to eat to keep up with the day.

All the trimmings of an authentic French breakfast had us drinking Mimosas and singing Sinatra songs. "It had to be you." He loved to sing this song, even when he didn't know the words. It really didn't matter much because I knew where his heart was and where we would be later that evening.

"Darling, I am to run an errand real quick back at my place. I told a designer to meet me close to my place, which is close to the furniture market, so she could show me some fabric samples for our new sofas and dining room chairs. This should only take about an hour, and I will be back over here very soon."

Chapter Seventeen

My one-bedroom apartment was located right in the heart of the Upper East Side. I knew when I moved into the Condo in the sky I would rent my place until my lease was up. I finished breakfast and, with everything I needed, kissed the Baron, and out the door I went. This was going to be an adventure. "I will meet you back here in an hour, so enjoy your coffee and breakfast, and I will see you shortly." Sealed with a kiss.

I walked east toward my apartment and felt a little happier once out the door. The weather was seasonally cold for New York this time of year; with the snow sticking to the ground, you knew it was cold out there.

I entered my building, and the doorman smiled and said, "Well, well... look who is coming in. Where in the world have you been traveling this time?" I laughed and said, "I am over on Fifth Avenue and having a holiday here in New York City."

Laughing to myself, I walked over to the elevators to take a ride up to the fifth floor, where my modest apartment was basically a large closet with lots of treasures, including my two dogs. I used Carol to watch my little guys on any given day and night. She was like a family member to me and the dogs. I put on sneakers so I could run up and meet the interior designer across the street from the Furniture Mart in a small cafe. "Hello, Susan. I am so happy to meet up with you and have you show me some samples."

She was originally from Houston but loved New York, so she came here to pursue her passion. I knew she was the girl for me when she joked about fixing to get a coffee and asked me if I'd like one. That was a Texas way of saying, I am going to get a coffee.

"I would love a latte with vanilla and extra cream." She proceeded to wait for the coffee, and I took a look at her samples as she had instructed. I knew the colors that came to mind when I picked up the swatches. I thought to myself, "Now, this is going to be a fun job in and of itself."

As she walked with two coffees, I asked how she liked living here in New York. "It's not Texas up here, but it is exciting. I am having my best life living here. I don't miss Texas at the moment, but I am sure I will go home after a few years."

"You never know when love walks in; you just might stay."

"I have a few minutes to share my goals for the Condo on 84th Street with you."

She looked down at the notes and began to write them as fast as she could to stay up with me. I really appreciated her participation in my project.

This was going to be a few months of working with her to create a masterpiece for us to enjoy in our new home. "We are closing on Tuesday of this week, so after we get the keys, I will have you meet me there for you to measure everything." She nodded and smiled back at me.

"I must leave now so I may return to my love waiting for me at St. Regis."

"Sounds like a plan, so I will have more things for you to look at, and we can meet up after Thanksgiving."

"Perfect." I grabbed my things and went out to hail a cab back to the hotel.

The traffic was extra heavy for some reason, not sure, but maybe with the holiday travelers in for Thanksgiving.

I knew the Baron would be here for another two weeks, so we would make it part of the program. Today, we had lunch at our favorite Italian restaurant, and tonight we are going to hear the man, the legend, Frank Sinatra. As the cab pulled up to the Hotel, I paid the driver and went up to the room where I would grab the Baron. We would just walk there from our hotel. Some sightseeing would be good for us, not to mention the exercise. After lunch, we will be able to walk off lunch and shop in some of my favorite shops along the way back. We walked into Cipriani with a large appetite and were ready for a Bellini or two.

"Good day. We have a reservation for two."

"Follow me" We walked around to the corner seat, where he sat us with two menus. A room with a view of people watching. The crowd seemed very young and beautiful.

This was a perfect mix for the afternoon. We couldn't wait for the waiter to bring us our Bellinis. "Good afternoon. May I start you both off with a couple of Bellini's?"

"Yes, let's have that and antipasti to start things off for us."

This was going to be a fantastic lunch with the Baron. We were here for the drinks and the view. "Excuse me while I go to the girl's room." He stood up and pulled my chair out. As I approached the bathrooms, my oldest boyfriend, Jack, walked out of the men's room. He smiled at me, walked up, and gave me a kiss on the lips.

A long-awaited kiss from my special friend. He was the first guy I fell in love with in New York, and we would always be connected. "What a surprise to see you here, sweetheart!"

"Who are you here with, Katherine?"

He took my breath away, so after I reconnected to the planet, I responded, "I am here with my new boyfriend."

"You know that I will always love you."

"I will, too."

"Take care of yourself."

"You too, sweetheart."

I walked into the bathroom and couldn't believe how he still made me feel. I walked back to the table and smiled at the Baron, who was delighted to see me. Across the way to my right was Jack, sitting there staring at us.

He made me blush tremendously. After all these years, I could still love that man and keep it at a distance. I turned my attention to the Baron. "Here is to us, my love. May this day be a postcard moment for us."

"Cheers."

The waiter took our order for lunch, and we sipped on our Bellini while we engaged in a sexy afternoon conversation. My eyes were always circling back around to Jack.

He had a piece of my heart and always would for the rest of the time.

"I just love this restaurant, darling."

I smiled with a nod. The first course came out along with another Bellini. I could feel this would be a liquid lunch more than anything. Everything smelled divine and tasted amazing. The flavors in the salad delighted my senses on every level, and I waited for the next course to be delivered. As I looked over to Jack's table, he and his friend were leaving their table. He looked over at me with a very sexy wink and a kiss to go. I thought of how much I loved that man, and he probably didn't even know it. That was fine for the moment. I thought back to when I had met him. Our first meeting was at a nightclub one night. His friend was walking behind me and tapped me on the shoulder, and said, "You want to meet the nicest guy you will ever meet in your life?"

I thought that must mean something, or that was one hell of an opening line. He turned around and smiled that smile with his dimples and melted my heart at that moment in time. I will never forget that moment or him.

We shared so many great times all over the world. Our time together might be later in life. We had a connection that so few have ever got the chance to experience. At the moment, I had one focus to concentrate on: my love for the Baron. We were finishing our lunch when the dessert tray arrived, and without even a blink of an eye, we ordered the tiramisu. It was so delicious here. Homemade every day and with all the right ingredients. "Darling, would you like any coffee?"

"Yes, a cappuccino would be perfect with this dessert."

"Waiter, we will have two cappuccinos, please."

Complete satisfaction at lunch with all the things that excite one's desires. An old lover, a new love, great cuisine, and off to shop at my favorite store across the street. What a great day to be alive, and then later off to hear' Ol' Blue Eyes,' and possibly some hot erotic sex later. Who could ask for anything more? We finished up, and while the Baron paid the bill, I checked my phone, and there was a sweet text from Jack. "A big kiss and a whole lot of love to you, my precious girl."

That excited me and had me daydreaming about him, so I turned it off. The phone and my mind from wandering down memory lane. I knew that we would see each other again real soon. "Thank you for dining with us this afternoon."

"Until we meet again, my friend."

We walked out of the restaurant and headed across the street to do some shopping.

Life was grand today on every spiritual level. Love was connecting us to a beautiful realm of possibilities. Where the day would continue to take us was anyone's guess, but I couldn't wait to feel the passion from the energy surrounding us. Once inside the store, I knew just where to go. Ride the escalator up to the second floor, which was the shoe department. The gorgeous display of the most expensive designer shoes on the planet.

A girl always needs a new pair of shoes, and this place had everything you could dream of in every color, shape, and size.

"What shoe are you in the mood for, darling?" This was going to be fun.

"I am not sure exactly which way to go or where to start." I knew that it would be a high heel, but not sure which designer. I walked around and picked up several shoes that I liked. After finding one I loved, we had the woman ring it up, and off we went to find a dress for the night.

Chapter Eighteen

It was beginning to all come together. Dress and shoes in hand, now down to the first floor for a handbag. "Darling, you are a woman after my own heart. You shop quickly and know exactly what you like and what looks good on you." He never asked for the price of each item.

I found the right bag to go with the shoes and the dress. "We are done, and it only took us an hour or less. Let's get ready for this evening."

"A glass of champagne sounds good to me, darling. How about you, my love?"

"Let's go get it all."

We only had to walk a few blocks to our hotel, so we had plenty of time for a drink or two.

"Let's have our packages sent up to the room while we have a drink."

Once inside, we left them with the front desk, and they would see to it that they were sent up before we arrived.

"I am so appreciative of your kindness and good taste in fashion, darling." I knew that he had just spent

several dollars on my new items. It meant the world to me to be spoiled for the moment. I never took him for granted or even thought about it. His generous attitude was just that, and it was exciting.

"I would like to go up to the room and start getting ready, my love."

He seemed fine with me going up without him. "I am coming up with you, darling. Let me get the bill, and I'll be right up."

After taking my shower and preparing my makeup for tonight, I poured myself a glass of champagne.

"I hope you are ready to see the man, the legend." He kissed me as he walked by. "We have a fun night ahead of us, and with a little luck and a lot of love, we will knock it out of the park.

"Are we ready to go see Franky, baby?" He smiled at me, and it always melted my heart. "Darling, are you ready to go downstairs?"

I replied, "I need five more minutes, darling. I'll be right there."

So, he waited in the parlor, listening to Frank Sinatra and getting ready for the evening. We were planning to grab a quick dinner before the show, which is at Radio City Music Hall. "I am ready." I walked out of the bedroom with the most beautiful, elegant outfit on, my new earrings and the beautiful pearl necklace that the Baron had given me.

"Shall we go then, my love?"

"Yes, let's go."

We rode the elevator down, singing Frank songs all the way.

We didn't have far to go, so the concierge had picked an elegant restaurant for us before the show. Our driver was waiting for us in the car. Once inside the car, we told him we wanted to go to the Four Seasons restaurant and that the concierge had made a reservation. Upon our arrival, he asked us who we were going to see this evening.

I answered, "We are going to see Sinatra. You wanna go?"

The driver said, "Thank you very much. I appreciate the offer, but I'm going to stick with driving you both tonight."

He was a happy soul and always had a smile on his face. We were seated upon arrival and knew we only had an hour for dinner.

"Darling, I think we should order the mussels to start."

"I love that idea, my love. I'll have a salad to follow, and that's enough for me."

We ordered our meal along with a bottle of champagne. We even had a chocolate souffle for dessert. "How was that for a quick and easy dinner?"

"Perfect."

We headed for the car when I noticed our friend Ana at the bar. She was with a guy that looked familiar.

The closer we got to them, the crazier it was that she was sitting there with a good friend of mine. He was a young, handsome restaurant guy. He owned a few spots around town, and we had a history together.

"Hey Ana, it's good to see you."

He looked at me, a bit shocked. I introduced him to the Baron, and Ana jumped up and hugged him. I leaned over and pinched my friend. He laughed at me, and we acted like we didn't know each other. Playful and sexy at the same time.

"Well, we are headed over to hear Frank Sinatra, so we will see you guys later." I winked at him while hugging her goodbye. See you later. We walked down the staircase and outside to get into our car.

"*Darling, how did you know that gentleman with Ana?*"

"*We run in the same circle of friends. We have mutual friends here in the city, and I've seen him around town.*"

I really didn't know what to say to him to comfort him. I guess he could tell the attraction between us was there and pretty strong. "*We are here, my love. Let's go have some fun listening to ole blue eyes.*"

Our seats were several rows back from the stage. Perfect seats!

"*Darling, we scored perfect seats to hear our favorite singer.*"

As the lights went down and the curtains went up, the crowd started clapping as the music started playing. Right off the bat, the first song was "Fly Me to the Moon." We sang every word and kissed each other like school kids. Next up was "Witchcraft." All the songs we loved, one right after another were played for two straight hours, then he took a break and went up for a drink at the bar. "*Let's get some champagne upstairs.*"

"*What do you think about the show so far, darling?*"

I said without missing a beat, "I am absolutely loving Frankie. It's everything I thought it would be and then some."

As we got our two champagnes, we walked over and looked at the view from the windows of the New York skyline. "Magnificent City, New York, my love." The bells started to chime, which meant drinking up and heading back to your seat. We cheered on each other and drank up. Walking back, we threw our glasses out and found our seats just in time. The lights started to dim right as we landed in our seats. The curtain came up, playing our song. "It had to be you." We smiled and kissed each other while singing along. "No one else gave me a thrill but you."

"I love you, darling."

Smiling with a sexy smirk, I said, "I love you too, my love." The music played, and we sang all the songs together. Finally, it was time for New York, New York. "Sing it out loud, darling."

"New York, New York, to the city that never sleeps. These vagabond shoes are longing to stray."

We sang it till the very end. Then it was extra singing of New York. What a spectacular concert we just encountered! The crowd didn't want to leave, and neither did we, so we kept singing till the curtain finally went down.

"Darling, let us visit our watering hole and sing with Michael."

We called our driver to find his location and walked right to him. We jumped in the car and headed over to sing with Michael. "I only live to love you, darling." He held my hand while we rode across town, telling me he never wanted to leave me alone in New York. "I don't want you to be lonely, darling."

I smiled at him and rubbed his hand, whispering to him, "I just love you, darling. You've got a piece of my heart." We pulled right up to the front door of our favorite sing-along bar. "Let's fall in love even more than we already are, my love." I stepped out of the car and remembered my phone was on the seat. I turned back and grabbed it. Once inside, we made our way over to the piano, where Michael was playing all the great hits. "Hello, guys," said Michael. "How's it going?"

We answered, "Great. We came to see you and sing along to our favorite songs."

He smiled at us, and I winked back. "What do you guys want to hear first?"

The Baron immediately yelled to him, "It had to be you." Michael began to sing the song, and we joined in at that moment. Dancing and singing were my favorite things to do with him. We stayed there for another hour and closed the place singing, dancing, drinking, and celebrating life together.

We walked home to the Hotel, and we were madly in love with each other, celebrating our love for each other, and fell fast asleep. A long day full of memories that would be forever treasured in my heart. As dawn broke over the city of New York, a gorgeous sunrise was upon me. I made a cup of coffee in the room and ordered the continental breakfast for the two of us, and I let him sleep in as I thought about the things we were getting ready to do for the day.

We were going to look at furniture. We had to go up to the apartment and take measurements for everything. Our new doorman would let us in because tomorrow we would be closing on the Condo, as we didn't officially own it yet, and had to ask permission from the building. The door attendants at the new Condo building loved us. As I looked across the skyline, I was reminded of how much I was beginning to miss Buttons. His smile, charming personality, and all that attracted me to him. I wondered what he was up to but knew not to reach out to him because of where I was in my life at the time. I thought on his birthday in December, I would surprise him after the Baron leaves New York.

These feelings I had for him were strong, but I continued to suppress them. It wasn't the right time for us yet. However, being in love with Mr. Right at the wrong time was the theme of that tune. I focused on the now with the Baron and felt alive for the moment.

"Bon jour, Moi Cheri" was heard from the other room.

"Good morning, darling. Would you like your coffee there, or will you join me out here?"

"I will join you there in just a few."

I knew that I was experiencing a magical, once-in-a-lifetime romance. "I slept so well, my love, and I only hope that you did as well."

He smiled at me while tasting his first sip of morning coffee. I would wait for his answer after he woke up a bit more. I knew today was a big day for us. We were scheduled to close on the Condo in the sky around 11 a.m. This was going to be a very exciting day for us in our future as a couple. This would seal the deal for me, as he is the man and claims to be around me.

"Darling, why don't you head into the bedroom for a minute? I have a surprise for you!"

"I'm coming in there now."

I closed the door behind me, as I should have due to the lovemaking that was getting started here. Now, this is the way to start the day: with sexy lovemaking and then a hot bubble bath.

"You are one hot lover." I kissed him and went off to a bath to start this beautiful and loving day.

"We need to be downstairs around 10:30, my love, with bells and smiles on our faces."

He went to make a call to his Banker and several other people while I walked into the bathroom to have a hot bubble bath. I started my bath and poured just enough bubbles into the water. This would be one of the best hot baths ever.

Soaking in the bubbles with music from the speakers inside the bathroom made me so relaxed that I almost fell asleep. I was up and ready for the day. I chose a beautiful suit for the closing, a matching bag, and high-heeled shoes. Ready, Set, Go! Here we come! He jumped in the shower, and I poured myself another cup of coffee while he got ready for this very special day. I saw a text from Buttons on my phone, looking for me. This was not the day to respond, so I ignored the text. I didn't want anything to ruin this day for us.

We had worked so hard to get to this day, and nothing or no one would spoil this moment.

"How do I look, darling?"

"I thought you were a Hollywood Movie Star, my love. You look so handsome." I kissed him with a lot of passion.

"It is time to buy our Condo in the sky. Let's meet our future." We headed to the car, and along the way, the Concierge greeted me with the week's itinerary for dinner reservations and the Thanksgiving Day parade schedule.

"Thank you so much for spotting us on the way out the door." She smiled and nodded her head toward us. We greeted our driver and thanked him for waiting for us. "Good morning." We acknowledged him, and off we went to our closing. We would be signing all of the papers at his Bank in Midtown. A Swiss Bank held the majority of his money and would be helping with today's closing. This was going to be fun for everyone involved in today's transaction.

"We should be finished in a few hours, so we might just walk back after we decide where to have

lunch. A celebration is in order, so I will call you when we are in need of your service."

He wished us luck and, with a nod, said Goodbye. We walked inside the building and stopped at the front desk to show our ID and sign in. The Baron signed in, and we were handed badges for our visit. I jumped into the elevator and pushed the button to the 22nd floor. Once the doors closed, I kissed my lover in the elevator.

This was going to be a big day for both of us, and our future of taking the keys to our new Condo in the sky would be so exciting, yet all the things we had to look forward to were more exhilarating on every level. Once inside the office, we were greeted by the girl at the front desk, who instructed us to head back to the third door on the left, where there were books and pens, along with bottles of water and Champagne on the table. I eyed the Champagne in a beautiful French Silver Ice bucket, along with four tall Champagne Flutes. I recognized them because I had just bought them a French brand of elegant crystal stemware, silverware, and Fine China. I had started planning the look for the inside of our new Condo. I didn't have that beautiful French Silver Ice Bucket added to our collection of must-have things yet, so I looked it up online and ordered it. We would pick it up on our way to the Condo. The meeting was about to start once everyone took their seats. Two very attractive gentlemen walked into the room with lots of folders and books for us to sign and for them to register. This was also going to be educational for me to watch for future purchases in my life.

Chapter Nineteen

This was my first experience purchasing Real Estate here in New York City, and an impressive first condo to purchase, if I may add. "Good afternoon, everyone, and Welcome to the closing. We will review everything you both need to know before signing a mountain of documents. Please feel free to ask any questions if you need to; we will also have a French interpreter for you. Let's begin, shall we?"

I looked over at the Baron, and he smiled back at me with a lot of love. This was a magical postcard moment for us.

The words became a song to me with a French theme, one only Charles Aznavour could sing. A love story that would be read about later in life. The paperwork was signed, the documents were completed, signed, and delivered to the owners and their Bankers, and we had the keys in our hands.

"Congratulations to both of you." They opened the bottle of Champagne and poured us all a glass. The handsome gentleman who was in charge of getting everything signed raised his Champagne flute and

announced that we were the new owners of a beautiful condo on the Upper East Side. "I want to celebrate and congratulate the Baron and Kathrine on their new purchase. May the future be bright, and may you both always enjoy the views. If you need anything, we're here for you."

The Baron stood up and toasted the team. "I want to thank everyone here, in this room, for making me the happiest man alive today. Also, thank you to my darling, who has brought so much love into my life."

We all thanked him right back and drank up the last sips of our Champagne before exiting the room with all our paperwork, documents, and keys to our new Condo in the sky. "I am the happiest girl in the world." I leaned over and kissed him right on the lips.

"Where would you like to go for lunch?"

"Let's grab lunch across the street at a quaint little French restaurant for lunch."

The perfect place to continue the celebration was my first impression. As we walked over, the phone rang, and it was our driver asking if we needed him. "No, not at the moment, but I could use your service in about an hour."

We walked in, and they immediately sat us in the main room. The team had called ahead, reserved us the best seat in the house, and left a message that they were buying lunch. Well, let's eat up and order another glass of Champagne.

As we sat there, a Champagne silver bucket with ice and a bottle of Champagne arrived. The waiter asked us if we were ready for a glass of Champagne. "We are always ready for Champagne." This was going to be a fabulous lunch with Caviar and Champagne at the front of the meal. "Good afternoon. We have been told to bring out the best of the best for you both." They started us off with a large caviar and all the trimmings, along with two Caesar Salads.

Next, we had a beautiful filet of soles and two plates. Dessert was a key lime pie with two folks. "Darling, let's get wild and go back to our room after lunch. I am feeling so passionate for you." Bill Please!! We both looked at each other with that loving feeling. We asked for a bill, and nothing was owed. That is an amazing experience with a free lunch with only the very best items, including a very expensive bottle of bubbles. Now, getting back to the room would be a challenge. The Baron called for the driver to come pick us up and deliver us back to the Hotel.

He was waiting outside the restaurant because, after getting to know us, he knew we would need a ride. Once inside the car, we told him to take us back to the hotel where we had had a wonderful afternoon and started enjoying the finest Champagne and eating caviar and everything under the sun they could bring us. Still, we had just closed on our Condo in the sky, and we were going home to take a bit of a siesta so that we could be ready for the evening. We had dinner reservations for four because we were taking Carol and Charlie, whom we were celebrating Thanksgiving with tomorrow, to their home.

***

"Well, you must be starving by now." Just at that moment, Maria brought the largest plate of eggs, bacon, a stack of pancakes, home fries, and orange juice. Then, she turned around and went to get the pot of coffee to make sure he had fresh coffee. "What a breakfast!" This would be enough for them for the day until lunch or even an early dinner.

"What'd you think up to this point, Brian?" He looked a bit determined to eat and tell Grandma Kathrine his feelings at the same time.

"Grandma, I'm wondering how you felt about Buttons at that moment, if you missed him? Have you had any contact with him? Where did you stand with him while you and the Baron bought a condo?"

This would have been a lot for him to have taken, considering that he couldn't afford to do those things at present, nor was he ready.

"Brian, I was wondering if you would want to go do a little shopping in town for some items that I can give you as a gift for me from around here. It is up to you. We can go to the beach, or we could go for a sail. I have a friend who has several different types of boats. We can either go on a fast boat, a speedboat, or a sailboat. It depends on the weather today, but maybe getting out on the water might be a good thing for us. Let me call him up and see what he says about my idea. I will be right back." While she was out of the room, this gave Brian time to go take a shower and put some clean clothes on. He was thrilled to think of getting on the water. "We are on for 1 p.m. at his boat dock."

He just lived down the street from us, so it would be a quick drive over. It sounds like a great afternoon plan. "I will get my things ready, and off we shall go," said Grandma Kathrine. Henry was ready to drive them over and wait for them.

"Come on, Henry, why don't you come with us? We will be back in an hour, and you will really enjoy the ride."

He didn't have to think about it for very long. He jumped on board with them, and they set sail from the boat dock that Nickolas had built. Nickolas was an interesting guy that Grandma Kathrine had met in New York in the day. She believed he always loved her but never made a move on her, only a friendship. He organized a beautiful day on his sailboat, and with any luck and a lot of love, they would be sailing with the wind currents that seemed to be in their favor. Nickolas said to all of them, "Welcome aboard the EZ LIVING. She is a very comfortable 60-foot custom Sailboat designed in Maine."

This was some boat to see, and to have the privilege of sailing on it was incredible. Everyone just sat back and took in the fresh saltwater and sunshine. He had a full staff of young people serving cocktails and snacks for all of them. "Brian, what are your favorite memories of this beautiful lady you call Grandmother?" He smiled and drank a sip of his white wine.

"My fondest memories are being created as we sail. Thank you, Nickolas, for your warm hospitality towards us and for helping create one of the best days I have ever had with my grandmother."

They all smiled at each other, and then it was time to return home, for the weather was changing in just a few hours. The winds picked up, and they sailed back in ahead of the storm, which was brewing out in the ocean.

Once back at the docks, they all toasted to Nickolas. "Here is to Nickolas for an amazing day with my very handsome grandson, my dearest guy Henry, and my oldest friend from the good old days. Thank you for having us today and showing us a beautiful time out at sea." Nickolas came over, hugged her neck, and gave her a small kiss with a dip. "You haven't lost those old hot dance moves."

He was a very handsome guy back in New York. He owned several businesses but was best known for his way with girls. He always had a sweet spot for Katherine and kept in touch with her even after all these years. Some people enter your life and stay a part of it, no matter the distance or time that goes by.

Brian was the first one off the boat, but he thanked Nickolas before jumping off.

"Nickolas, darling, you still have a special place in my heart. I love you, my sweet friend. I will come to see you next week so we can fool around on this big boat."

He smiled and kissed her cheeks on both sides. He was originally from Greece and had the charming manners of a European Gentleman. "See you soon, sexy." That was their little way of flirting with each other. "Please be my guest tonight at my Greek Restaurant."

Grandma Kathrine looked at him with a smile and replied, "We would love to have dinner at your place." Brian's interest sparked at that point in the conversation. Henry drove them home to prepare for the evening. "I will be ready in an hour for dinner." Brian went his way to prepare for the evening, and Grandma Katherine went her way to get dressed for the evening. "Would you like a glass of wine while you get dressed?"

"Maria, please pour us a glass of our red wine. I'll take mine in my room."

They took off in separate directions, only to meet up in the same spot an hour later. "Brian, you are so handsome, like your father was so many moons ago. I know he must be extremely proud of the young man you've become today."

He looked up with a smile that melted her heart, just like his father used to do. "I am so happy to have this opportunity to spend such quality time with my best girl." That took me by surprise, and I just had to laugh out loud.

"That was your great-grandfather's best line on any given day. He was some kind of character, but I am sure you have heard everything about him."

That conversation was for a later date because tonight was about them. Henry offered to drive them, and Brian spoke up. "I'll drive us, Henry." He wanted to have that alone time with his grandmother. They loaded up in her Mercedes SUV and went off to South Beach. They arrived exactly 20 minutes later. "The Mediterranean awaits us, Brian."

The attendant opened their doors, and they got out, looking for the doors. The first thing that Grandma Kathrine experienced was the delicious smell of fresh everything. This was going to be a fun-filled evening for both of them.

The hostess greeted them and sat them down, overlooking the ocean. "This is some place, Grandmother."

At that time, the waiter walked up and smiled so big that Brian fell in love at first sight. "Good evening, everyone. My name is Cecilia, and I will be taking great care of you tonight. What can I get you started with this evening?"

"We will have a glass of your best Champagne. Thank you."

The views from their seats were spectacular and breathtaking, not to mention very romantic. The menu was straight from Greece, and the decor was that of the Island of Mykonos. Brian asked Grandma Kathrine to pick up where they left off with her story. "I am waiting to hear how you and the Baron celebrated your new Condo in the Sky."

She wasn't sure where to pick up her story, but she had a pretty good idea that after the extravagant lunch celebration and lovemaking back at the Hotel, the Baron and she would take a long nap.

***

I knew that once in a lifetime, you get to experience such bliss that I never wanted to let those feelings go from my memory, and neither would I with a little help from my grandson. We awoke from our nap with so much love in our hearts and a desire to get dressed for dinner and begin the celebration all over again, but this time with my dear friends, who had invited us for Thanksgiving. "Darling, may I kiss you all over?" This was the sexy part of the nap that only intrigued us. A kiss was only a kiss until your heart added an extra beat of pure happiness and the desire to make love. We had an extra special moment before jumping up to shower that would create a magical sexual moment. One experiences this kind of pleasure when the body, mind, and soul are connected and free. This would be how I felt that afternoon.

***

The waitress was flirting with him, and Grandma Kathrine could see it. "Here are the glasses of champagne that you ordered. Salute."

They toasted to the evening and sipped their first of many sips of champagne. "May your heart always allow love in and treasure it until the end."

They laughed at each other, and at that moment, she could tell that he got it.

"Ready to order your dinner this evening?" The cute waitress was back to smile at Brian and take their order. "Start us out with all the typical Greek dishes, then bring us an assortment of desserts to add to our experience." The plates kept coming until they didn't, and the champagne as well. This was quite a Greek experience. Everything tasted so delicious, and the entertainment started with music from the Greek Islands.

"What do you think about this restaurant?" She could tell that he really enjoyed the moment.

"Later on, they will pull the chairs together, and people will get up on the tables and dance on them."

Brian smiled really big and replied, "Will you be dancing, Grandma?" She stood up and started to dance in place. The energy in the place began to take on a nightclub feel.

Chapter Twenty

Watching his only Grandmother dance like she was 25 again was a remarkable experience for Brian. It was spectacular on all levels.

"I loved to dance back in the day, especially when I could jump up on these tables in my youth." As she reminisced about days gone by, Nickolas showed up at their table. "Good evening, my love."

He bent down to kiss her, and she kissed back. "You still got it, my love."

You could feel the passion between these two lovebirds. "Remember when we would dance all night and then head back to my place for breakfast?" asked Grandma Kathrine.

"We had more than just breakfast, doll."

Brian had to look away with a grin.

"Oh, la la, I can still remember those hot and steamy nights turned to sunrises."

Now, the table seemed a bit too sexy, and Grandma Kathrine had to excuse herself. "I'm going to powder my nose; excuse me."

Nickolas smiled at her with a little giggle. "I can still remember that being our code to meet in the little girl's room for a hot kiss. May I get you a fresh bottle of Champagne, doll?"

"Absolutely."

She walked off, and Nickolas turned to Brian and shook his head. "That is one classy lady, Brian. You are truly blessed to have her as your role model." He smiled down at him without words.

Brian looked back at him. "I know."

The music started to play the hot sounds of the Greek Islands, and before Grandma Kathrine returned from the restroom, they were pushing the tables together and clearing off the tablecloths. The waitress, Cecilia, was making her way to the table to ask if they needed anything else and to flirt with Brian. It was obvious that she found Brian handsome, and beyond a shadow of a doubt, there would be some hot dancing between them.

Nickolas turned to Grandma Kathrine. "You want to show these kids how it's done?" The most handsome guy in the place was the Owner.

"Absolutely."

They began to dance and found themselves dancing back in time. They had had chemistry from day one, and so many years later, it was still alive.

The art of making love was on the dance floor. If you could dance on the dance floor like you were making love, the rest would be sizzling hot in the bedroom.

"You still got the moves, Nickolas."

He kissed her and whispered, "You've still got it, babe."

As the song ended and another played on, Nickolas and her sat down, where he had a fresh bottle of champagne already opened.

"We danced like that more than 40 years ago."

They had smiles on their faces to light up the evening sky. That was just a moment in time for the both of them. Brian walked up and asked if they should start back home before they needed a driver. He wasn't drinking like his grandmother, so he was fine to drive.

"Thank you, Nickolas, for the amazing time tonight. The dinner was delicious, as was the service. I would love to ask Cecilia for her number if that would be okay with you."

Nickolas laughed, saying, "You don't need my blessing, boy; go ask her for her number."

Brian grinned. "I'll be right back with that number, and I will drive us home."

They needed to get home, for the excitement of it all had made Grandma Kathrine tired and ready to lie down. She was concerned that she needed to visit her Physician as soon as possible.

Tonight, was not the night to put a sadness or concern spell on them. Tomorrow would be another day to deal with her health issues, not tonight.

As Brian walked up with a smile on his handsome face, they all knew why, and with just a bit of luck, maybe this new friend would amount to something fun for him. "Goodnight, everyone."

They walked to the valet and gave him the ticket for their car. "I am so happy you met a nice girl tonight, Brian. You are one handsome young man, and with your genes from your father and grandfather, the girls will be lining up around the corner."

He laughed with the sheer innocence of the youthful boy about to embark on his manhood.

The car pulled up, the sweet valet boys opened their doors, and Brian tipped them both.

"You are a kind soul, Brian. Don't ever change because of outside forces."

He smiled back at his grandmother and continued driving the Mercedes SUV back home. Once inside, Grandma Kathrine took off for her room to freshen up and slip into something more casual to wear. She had enjoyed herself but felt a bit tired from all the activities in one day. Life had a funny way of showing you certain moments that completed the mystery of your life. This was true for her today. She knew that Nickolas and her would always feel a strong desire for each other. Once in a few years, the desire would create stimulation beyond a doubt. She was sitting on the couch in the living room when she saw Brian headed towards the kitchen. Smiling, she whispered, "Feeling like a midnight snack?"

She jumped up and joined him in the kitchen. "How did Thanksgiving go with the Baron?"

Brian wanted her to continue with the story. "Funny you mention that, sweetheart. I felt like bringing it up for your ears to hear the continuation of my fabulous love story."

***

Well, as one would think of a traditional Thanksgiving with all the family around and the trimmings of Turkey, our day was full of caviar and champagne. Really, is there any other way? If you asked me, it was a treat not to feel pressured into cooking, and at this time in my life, I wasn't cooking Thanksgiving dinner.

The day began with a little lovemaking, then a bath and breakfast in the room. A full pot of coffee and croissants for two, along with fruit and yogurt. I turned on the Macy's Thanksgiving Day Parade, which would be right outside our window for viewing, but watching it live on TV would be easier. A Thanksgiving tradition was to watch the Thanksgiving Day Parade with my mother every year. While she prepared the meal and planned according to the time, we would watch it together. So, we turned on the Parade while we enjoyed our breakfast. "Darling, I look forward to celebrating a traditional American holiday with you and your friends. This will be my first Thanksgiving in America."

That is something to think about for an American who has always celebrated this holiday. This was his first Thanksgiving.

I immediately responded, "You are a pilgrim to the party, my love."

You could feel the love in the room at this moment.

"Let's get dressed and be ready to head over to their apartment around 2 p.m."

I had the hotel kitchen prepare a dish that I could take over to share with everyone. They were watching my two dogs, so they felt like family to me. The energy was exciting for all involved to participate in a memorable Thanksgiving.

"Sweetheart, I am headed to the bathroom to prepare for our big day together."

I poured in the bubbles for my bath and stepped into the tub when it had plenty of water.

I sat there, sipping on my coffee, thinking of Buttons for just a split second. I knew he would be in Boston, enjoying his favorite holiday with his family. His sister celebrated her birthday a day after Thanksgiving, and his was a week later, so they would have a big celebration for both. His smile stayed in my heart for the entire day. I knew our day would come somewhere in the future if it was meant to be. I wanted it all to work out for everyone in its due time.

I was dressed and focused on the day ahead with my sweetheart. I really tried to live in the moment, with each day being a new day and a new adventure. Let's see what today will bring and how much fun awaits us.

"I will call for the car to pick us up after I have retrieved the items from the kitchen." The look on my sweetheart's face was that of someone just telling me where to go and at what time. As I gathered many items I wanted to take over to share with everyone, I picked up my purse and took the Baron's hand, and we went out of the hotel door. These would be days to remember for

everyone. Kissing each other took place once we got inside the elevator.

"Thank you for being here with me on this special holiday." He looked at me and gave me the most heartfelt kiss ever. "I love you, darling."

Just then, the elevator doors opened, and we walked up to the Concierge, where a special bag was ready for us. "Bonjour."

The woman replied back with Bonjour. "Happy Thanksgiving to you. Do you have our special request ready?"

She smiled back and handed me the bag on her desk. "This bag is for you both to take to your dinner." I smiled at her and offered a big thank-you. Less work for me. I enjoyed having it pre-ordered and ready to serve. This would be a terrific dish for everyone to enjoy today. "Thank you again." We walked outside and down the steps to our driver, who was waiting to drive us across town for our Thanksgiving dinner.

"Happy Thanksgiving, Frank." We both jumped in the car and spoke those kind words to Frank, our driver for the day.

"This is my first Thanksgiving, Frank." The Baron proclaimed.

"Happy Thanksgiving, then, to you." He began to drive us across town to Carol and Charles's apartment.

What an incredible feeling one experiences on Thanksgiving, and this being his first experience, it melted my heart for him. "Darling, thank you for being you and for loving me with all your heart."

The moment of compassion for another being embodied me, and what an amazing feeling to have, especially on this day.

We arrived at the apartment building, and Frank pulled up to the front doors. "Have a happy day, and I will be here to drive you back to the Hotel."

"Thank you, my friend." We proceeded to jump out of the car, and Frank stood there helping us out of the car. The building had a doorman who quickly escorted us up to my friend's place. Once the elevator doors opened, you could smell Thanksgiving and all its trimmings.

We knocked on the door, which was slightly opened for us due to the doorman calling them to announce our arrival.

"Happy Thanksgiving, guys." We walked into a celebration of friends and family gathered around the

kitchen.

"Hello, guys, and Happy Thanksgiving," Carol said from the dining room.

"Happy Thanksgiving, Carol."

They were setting up the table for us to be seated, and I noticed the beautiful flowers on the table, which reminded me to ask if she had received the flowers that we sent her.

"These flowers are magnificent, Carol."

Without hesitation, she replied, "Thank you for sending them to us. We really appreciate them."

We had also brought two bottles of Champagne for Carol. "Here are some bubbles to toast with you and your family on this perfect Thanksgiving celebration. Thank you for having us today. This is the Baron's first Thanksgiving, and I appreciate your warm and kind hospitality."

Carol opened one of the bottles of Champagne and asked me to help pour it into crystal flutes. I handed them out, and we toasted our friendship and our day together.

"Everyone step into the dining room and find your seats for our Thanksgiving dinner together."

We walked towards the table and approached our seats, where we found our names in front of our plates. A very elegant style of serving us Thanksgiving. Carol announced that we were starting off with the caviar that the Baron and I brought to kick off the Thanksgiving meal. Why not, if you feel like it? Which was never a question for me.

"Wonderful touch to our dinner," Carol mentioned that she had Caviar with us for the Baron's birthday last month and how much we enjoyed it.

"These two eat Caviar like we eat pizza." Everyone laughed.

Her son and his girlfriend were at the table, and her niece from DC, who was studying at Georgetown University, brought her boyfriend to the Thanksgiving celebration. There were eight people in total sitting around the Thanksgiving table, enjoying the moment.

We brought enough Caviar for an Army, so no worries; we wouldn't be short on anything. "I hope everyone likes caviar and champagne. It is our favorite appetizer with any meal. I would like to Thank Carol and Charles for having us celebrate this American tradition."

A big hug to both of them, along with a hug to the Baron for being here with me on this occasion. Charles was a comedian with a very creative mind and a musician at night. He played in a rhythm and blues band. They performed all over the city and would travel to special events. They had a very old-school sound to them.

"Charles, where have you been performing lately?"

He smiled and replied, "My band has been down in New Orleans for the Jazz Festival, and I just finished doing stand-up comedy at a local club."

Everyone seemed excited to hear him perform; whether it was music or joketelling, we were all ears. "I'll play my guitar for you if you would like after dinner."

We all smiled and agreed that after dinner would be perfect.

The caviar and champagne went quickly, and the main course was headed to the table. Carol had hired a full staff to help with everything for the day, allowing her to engage with her guests. They were a tremendous help with just about everything that day. I asked for their contact information for future parties at our new place.

The turkey and dressing had landed on the table, along with prime rib and ham. The sides were on every corner of the table, and a new bottle of champagne arrived just in time. The amount of food at our table was insane, to say the least. Everyone seemed to be enjoying themselves, and the background music gave the room a cool vibe.

Chapter Twenty-One

It was a perfect Thanksgiving for the Baron to experience. Once the forks had landed perfectly across the plates and the last mouthful had been dissolved, Charles began playing music in the other room. We simply left our seats at the table and walked across the hall to find a spot on the sofa to listen to the beautiful sounds of Charles.

"Thank you to each of you for contributing to our Thanksgiving Day celebration."

He could play the guitar and sing as well. We stayed and listened for about an hour, then excused ourselves and bowed out gracefully.

"We had an amazing time today, and thank you again for showing me how a true American holiday is to be celebrated."

We hugged and kissed our way out of there while I arranged for our driver to pick us up. The elevator arrived and took us down to the lobby to greet the doormen. We walked to our car, jumped in, and headed across town to our hotel.

"What a wonderful day we had to celebrate Thanksgiving."

I could tell the Baron was content and ready for the night to have some bedroom fun. Bedroom fun was exactly what I had in mind for our last event.

"Darling, can we just head directly to our room and spend the last moments of the day loving one another?"

A huge smile wrapped around his face, and no words were necessary. Our room was the only place on my horizon that I wanted to see. While walking into our room and spotting the bed, I could only think of jumping in and calling it a night.

"Darling, I know you delighted me with a sexual encounter, but let's just jump into bed and cuddle one another. You never know what might come from the love connection we feel in that bed."

We both agreed through our eyes that this was the game plan. Once inside the bedroom, a certain kind of love surrounded the energy in our space. We began kissing each other as if it were the first time. He started to undress me as I started to undress him. The lighting produced a lovely, enchanting atmosphere.

The warm, glowing, and dimmed lights were just enough to tickle your imagination with the idea of hot lovemaking. "It had to be YOU, my love." We both said those words to each other at the same time. The moment had arrived that warmed my soul and made me want more. "My love for you is only getting stronger day by day and night by night."

My heart was full of love at this moment for the Baron. He had surprised me with how emotional he was with me. We found a love that doesn't come along very often, if at all. We embraced each other, knowing this love was pure and natural. The night turned into an intimate one, with our hearts full of love as we went off to sleep. "Goodnight, Darling."

The morning sun beamed brightly into our room from the East window and woke us up for breakfast. A ring was at the door, and with great surprise, we had all the goodies that we enjoyed on the table.

"May I place this in your room?" the kind man said without a beat.

"Yes, of course, but I am unsure when we ordered this breakfast." Then it hit me that we had left the order on the door before bed.

"Oh yes, now I remember."

He wheeled breakfast in and left it in the hallway.

The fresh smell of coffee had me following the tray.

"May I pour you a cup of coffee, darling?"

With a big smile, he replied, "Please, my darling."

While pouring the coffee, I couldn't help but go over in my head the course of yesterday for us. Two coffees later and a basket of croissants, fresh fruit and Greek yogurt, my body thanked me for feeding it a wicked hangover.

"Darling, I believe we were overserved on Thanksgiving."

He laughed so hard that it made me start laughing at myself. "I know who overserved us—me." Now, that was funny. The quiet moments in the morning with him were my most memorable, to say the least.

"What do you feel like doing today, darling?" My eyes lit up with excitement at the thought of having a free day to wander the streets of NYC. So today would be a fun day to shop, eat, and drink. Maybe Ice Skate at Central Park or take a horse and carriage ride.

The day was ours to explore this great city. My favorite city besides Paris that I have ever lived in to date, I wanted to show him a secret garden that I knew of in the park, along with a lunch fit for a King and Queen. Maybe the Met for a quick view of the Masterpieces, then a bit of shopping for an outfit to wear for dinner tonight. I had booked dinner for us at our favorite spot close to our Hotel, Le Cirque, and I was never disappointed. There you had it—a day full of adventure, love, and beauty. This would be a November day to remember.

"Darling, I have our day planned. You are going to love today. I am calling it a November day to remember."

He looked over at me with pure love in his heart. You could feel it. "Well, I am off to get ready to begin this magnificent day. Excuse me."

We both went our separate ways to prepare for our day together in NYC. This would be an index card memory. I turned on the bathtub and poured a little extra bubble bath. I pulled my hair up and left it up all day because I wanted a more sophisticated look for today. I knew just the dress and jacket I wanted to wear, along with the perfect flat shoes to dress it up. I would pick out the bag, and off we would go. This was going to be the most perfect day with the Baron. He dressed quickly, and

I prepared myself within a few minutes. "Darling, you look perfect for our magical day. I love your hair up and away from your face. Shall we take a photo to capture the best November day ever?"

"Yes, darling," I said with sheer excitement. I grabbed the camera, set the timer, and ran and jumped in the photo. "Here's to our best day ever."

The camera took our photo, and away we went to start our adventurous day. Two beings in love off to explore an amazing city with passion and love. We both had a kick in our step and lots of love in our hearts, feeling free to accept whatever the day brought our way. Once the elevator doors opened to the bottom floor, we walked out of the Hotel to begin the day. The sunshine was beaming so bright on the buildings, the reflection was insanely bright. The color of the Sky was Ocean blue, and the weather was brisk throughout your body. "I am glad that we have gloves, darling."

We walked hand in hand north to the park. Once we crossed the street, we walked along Fifth Avenue up to the Central Park Zoo. We glanced at all the animals while walking through the Secret Garden. It was just outside the gates of the Zoo.

A children's park was on the right side, with a giant slide that was created out of rock and little Forts and Swings for kids of all ages. "Darling, this is my secret garden. I plant seeds every year, and beautiful flowers bloom in the Springtime."

He smiled back at me and said, "I love that you've made this space in this large park your SECRET GARDEN."

I bought a bench and donated it to the park for all those like myself to sit and admire the beauty of the Spring flowers. It was engraved, "SIT AWHILE AND FEEL SPRING ALL YEAR ROUND." This made us both smile. He wrapped his arms around me and began to kiss me.

The long-awaited kiss "I love you, darling." Those words never grew old for me. I just loved being in love. Was there anything better? He took my hand, and we began to walk towards the Boat House, where we would have lunch. We were ready to run into the Metropolitan and view some amazing Art. The lunch began with a glass of bubbles, two salads, and a beautiful view of Central Park.

"Darling, this is a perfect spot for the two of us. Bon Moi Cheri."

I took that as a way to go, sweetheart, but in French. Our conversation never disappointed, and in such a romantic setting, we indulged in what would be his last lunch for a while. We looked at each other and began to flirt. We had that breathless attraction for each other that made us feel frisky.

Love was in the air, and we could feel it everywhere we looked. Couples kissing on a small boat in the middle of the lake, to kissing couples holding hands while walking through Central Park.

"Let's head up to view Art, darling." He paid the bill, and off we went to the Metropolitan Museum. It was only about seven blocks up Fifth Avenue, so we walked there on this beautiful day.

Once inside the museum, we checked our coats and proceeded to buy tickets. They had the Claude Monet Collection from Paris, which would excite me to no end, just to view the pieces I once viewed while living in Paris. All those beautiful memories flooded my head with such fondness, so I went up to the second floor to experience them with the love of my life. This moment felt so special beyond words at this point. We walked to the elevator and took it up to the second floor. The exhibit was directly in front of us, and with so many people observing the exhibit, we stood in line for a few minutes. Once inside the exhibit, love could be felt in every painting.

Every painting was more daring than the one before it. I enjoyed this moment tremendously and could have made love right there in the Museum. There is something very sexy about sharing the arts with the one you love, who also adores Art. This was the perfect November Day by far for any art lover, champagne drinker, cigarette smoker, or lovemaker; it didn't get much better than today, and we still had the night to go. We both celebrated our love for Monet, the founder of Impressionist paintings, with a stolen kiss just in front of my favorite masterpiece of his, Water Lilies.

"Darling, you are my true love," he said with a kiss on my cheek. "Let's go down and find the exit so we can head back to the Hotel."

I couldn't think of anything more desirable at that point in the day. We grabbed our things, the coat gal placed our coats on, and out the door we went. So many emotions stirred in my head that I needed a glass of champagne.

"Shall we finish up and head back to the Hotel?" He immediately asked if I wanted to go shopping.

"I have something special to wear for dinner tonight." We were in great shape as far as timing goes.

"Let's grab this cab, darling." He had hailed a cab by raising his hand in the air and signaling the cab to approach us on the right side of the street.

"Please take us to Tiffany's." The man started the meter, and off we went down Fifth Avenue.

"Why Tiffany's, my love?"

He replied quickly, "I want to purchase a small token of today's memory. Seal it with a piece from Tiffany's."

I am all in with that idea. "I will put you out on the far-right corner of 57th Street and Fifth Avenue." We both jumped out and walked towards the store. Once inside the store, the Baron knew exactly where to go. He had a piece in his mind already. "Darling, you love sapphires, right?"

My eyes focused on his eyes in disbelief. What in the world was he thinking of to just want to buy me a sapphire ring?

This was a spectacular ring, with diamonds on both sides of the sapphire. "Wow, darling, I am speechless."

The girl waiting on us, Melanie, had the biggest smile on her face for me. "What a beautiful ring, Madame."

My look back at her was pure love for my darling. I am so madly in love with this man.

"Darling, you just keep spoiling me, and I LOVE IT." He told Melanie I would wear that beautiful piece out but would love the box and Tiffany bag.

"Je t'aime, Darling."

We kissed inside Tiffany's as if nothing else in the world seemed to matter until it was time to get a room.

This was our little inside joke. We always laughed at people kissing in public and would joke about getting them a room. "This is just a small gift from me of the beautiful time we've spent together for Thanksgiving and the perfect November Day. I hope you will always smile and think of me when you see this ring looking back at you."

"Thank you from the bottom of my heart, darling. I am one lucky girl to have you in my life."

We thanked everyone for helping with this special occasion and headed for the exit on Fifth Avenue.

"Darling, let's go back to our hotel and celebrate at the bar with two Champagnes." They greeted us at the

front door of the St. Regis Hotel, where we would be celebrating the Christmas holiday together. Same suite along with the same people and then a few new ones. We would start taking things up to our new Condo in the Sky, but we wouldn't be able to stay overnight without the furniture. We would prepare to have furniture delivered and have all the services turned on in our names after the weekend. This would be an exciting time for us, without a doubt, as we start a new life together in our new CONDO IN THE SKY.

All of our dreams were happening so fast that we didn't have time to stop and think about them all, so we kept going, and one day, it would be a best seller. A story worth telling the world about just how magical this life was for one girl from Texas with big dreams and lots of love to give the world. As we walked towards the bar to have a glass of Champagne before our dinner tonight at our favorite restaurant in the city, we ordered a bottle of Champagne to take back to the room, saying,

"We will take that up to our room after we have one glass here, PLEASE."

The bartender pours us two glasses and corks the bottle with a fancy crystal stopper for us to take back to the room.

"To our love story, one for the storybooks and for our hearts to find happiness."

Cheers as we toast to each other. "Darling, you are the love of my life, my true love, and I want to spend my life with you."

I looked like a schoolgirl with love in her eyes for the first time.

"I agree, sweetheart. You are my sunshine on a cloudy day."

We embraced each other with a big kiss, and a hug followed. "Excuse me, darling, while I prepare for the most fabulous evening."

He smiled at me and said, "Take your time, my beauty Queen."

I dashed into the bathroom and started my bath with all the trimmings. Bath salts, bath bubbles, and my glass of champagne to continue with the celebration. Once I sat down inside the tub, my whole body began to relax, and I thought of Buttons and what he was up to for the evening. I could only imagine him out with his friends or up at his family home in Boston, but for a split second, he came inside my space and my head. It wouldn't stop me from enjoying myself in my bath, so I kept it to myself. I decided on a beautiful dress with shoes and a handbag to match. *"May I pour you another glass, darling?"*

The Baron asked, and I immediately answered, "Yes, my love."

I opened my door, all dressed and ready to celebrate the evening with the love of my life. Dressed in designer evening wear, followed by matching shoes and a bag, I had it ready for an evening in town in the big city. My handsome love walked out looking so charming and ready to celebrate as well. "Darling, you look so beautiful this evening. I hope you love your new ring from Tiffany's."

Without missing a beat, I answered, "I am in love with it like I am in love with you, my love."

We hugged each other and began to dance around the room, cheek to cheek. Our song started up and created a desire to be with each other.

"Do you spoil all the ladies like this, my darling?" He smiled at me with the most amazing smile. A smile that could be felt from deep down inside his soul, a place of pure joy. "I am going to grab my purse and coat, and then we should head to the car for dinner." We gathered our coats and walked to the elevator. I knew the Baron would be leaving tomorrow and we would be apart for a few weeks, so I wanted tonight to be extra

special. The elevator doors opened, and we took the elevator down to the lobby.

He hugged me and whispered, "I love you, darling."

As we looked into each other's eyes, I could feel time stand still without movement. "I love you too."

We walked outside and found our driver, who was waiting for us.

"Good evening, you guys." We jumped into the car, and our driver knew just where to take us. The hotel always gave him our itinerary ahead of time. "How are you love birds doing tonight?"

We looked at each other and gave each other the kindest kiss.

I felt that kindness would be our greatest attribute toward others. "We are more in love tonight than we have been since we met, darling." He grabbed my hand and smiled at me with so much love. "I've got you near my heart, darling."

Sealed with a kiss for the other. We arrived at the Restaurant for dinner with love in our hearts. We exited the car and walked up to the door, where a hostess greeted us. "Good evening and welcome."

They knew that we were coming, so they had our table ready with a glass of champagne ready for us. This was the way we liked to arrive at our favorite restaurant. Once we sat down, we raised our champagne flutes and toasted each other.

"Thank you for showing me so much love. I will miss you, my darling, but knowing we will be together in just a few weeks makes it easier. While we are apart, I will send you love letters that are straight from my heart."

I looked at him with pure love. "We will be together in spirit and reconnect stronger in love."

Chapter Twenty-Two

The waitress arrived to take our dinner and dessert order, a chocolate soufflé.

"Do you feel like caviar, my love?"

"ALWAYS." I would never say no to caviar.

"We will take your finest caviar and two spoons for dessert."

The waitress smiled back at us and proceeded to place our order. This would be our last meal shared until next month. "Darling, next month we will celebrate Christmas in New York, and where would you like to go for New Year's Eve, St. Bart's?"

I thought we would have a fabulous time celebrating New Year's Eve in St. Barts. "Sounds like a wonderful idea, my love."

"I will have my secretary book us the tickets from New York and reserve the best accommodations for us." The caviar arrived just as we needed another glass of champagne.

"Here you go, our finest caviar. May I pour you another glass of bubbles?" The waitress inquired courteously.

We looked at one another and agreed to another glass. "Please, we would love another glass of champagne."

We drank up and finished off the caviar, only to have our dessert arrive just in time. The feeling of love and all we had accomplished on this trip was almost overwhelming.

"Thank you for a delicious moment in time, darling." Smiles were felt by everyone.

"We are finished." The waitress brought our bill, and we concluded our dinner with a kiss.

"This was a beautiful way to end our time together," I sighed. We walked to the car and had our driver take us back to the hotel. We really just wanted to spend time together upstairs in our room on our last evening. "You have made me feel so young at heart and in my soul. I will always remember this moment in time." Once upstairs, we both decided to get out of our clothes and slip into something a bit sexier.

I dressed in a beautiful, sexy lingerie piece that he had bought for me. "How do you like my sexy lingerie?" I teased him.

He couldn't stop staring at me. "Oh, la la Moi Cheri!" I began to flirt with him and kiss his neck, which would lead us to experience an unforgettable sexual encounter. We couldn't stop kissing each other and feeling each other's love. We both fell asleep in each other's arms.

The morning sunlight awakened us to prepare for his departure. I also packed my bags with all my new outfits, along with all my new bags and shoes. We had breakfast sent up to us because the driver would be here to pick us up in an hour. The energy in the room seemed sober and a bit sad; we truly didn't want to be apart. "Darling, I must tell you that I am sad thinking of being without you for the next two weeks, but I know that when we reunite, it will be Christmas, literally." We kissed and embraced each other with so much love.

Picking up that last bag and heading downstairs to take the car out to the airport, we stopped, looked around, and said goodbye until we met again. The driver placed all our bags into the trunk of the car, and away we went to drop me off at my place.

"Take care of yourself, darling, and I will call you when I land in Belgium."

The car stopped, and I jumped out while the driver opened the trunk and handed my bags to me. My doorman ran out to help me with everything.

"I will miss you, my love," I said to him. We kissed, and he went to the airport. He turned back to wave at me, and we both could feel our hearts waving back.

Once inside my apartment, I unpacked my suitcase and sat on the sofa to catch my breath. All the visions of our time spent together were running a loop in my head. Every moment was so magical that I couldn't believe it all really happened. "Was it all just a dream, or was this my life?" I asked myself.

Just at that moment, the phone rang, and I immediately thought it was the Baron, but to my surprise, it was Buttons.

"Hey stranger, where have you been?"

I didn't know what to say. It left me speechless at that exact second.

I answered back, "Hey, handsome." Now, this was an odd feeling, being into another lover and yet wanting to see him at the same time.

"When can we get together? You know my birthday is on Thursday, and I was hoping to spend it with you."

I didn't know what to say to that proposition. "Let's figure it out and make a plan. Will you be in the city next week?"

I fumbled at every word spoken but somehow made it through the conversation. "I would love to celebrate your birthday with you. Where would you like to go for dinner?"

I thought, why not? I had two weeks till the Baron would return, and I wasn't going to sit around and be sad.

"Life is short, and there are too many men and so little time." This quote would be one I would live by on any given day or night. We hung up on plans to see each other in the city for his birthday on Thursday. The Baron called late at night to let me know he had arrived home safely and sound and was missing me already. I told him that I missed him too.

I spent the next few days preparing everything and working out each day. I needed to relax and shift gears for the next moment. It would be very exciting for me. I answered phone calls from many girlfriends wanting to know how everything was going in my life. Catching up with everyone was fun, and telling them all about my recent life events made it even more exciting. This was a once-in-a-lifetime kind of love, and I knew it to be true; however, I wasn't sure how my feelings were for Buttons or where we would find ourselves for his birthday. The days flew by, and I organized a beautiful dinner at a fun restaurant for him. A very romantic setting for our first date in quite some time. He called me the day before and asked where and when he should arrive at my place.

"Hey, birthday boy, how are you? I cannot wait to celebrate with you tomorrow."

He laughed on the other end and asked me to save him a dance. It had been a while since we had gone dancing, but I thought of how electrifying our bodies were on the dance floor. He and I could dance, and together, it was a sight to see.

"Meet me here at my apartment around 7 p.m., and we will go to the restaurant. The weather isn't going to be the best, so allow for time to get into the city."

He answered me, "I am working in the city tomorrow, so I can be there on time."

"Fabulous," I responded. This was shaping up to be a fun evening for us. I thought of what a sexy outfit I could coordinate for this evening. The perfect little black dress was always waiting to be worn with that perfect pair of heels, not to mention the black evening bag to match.

So, it was all set, and plans were arranged for a birthday celebration for Buttons. It was hard to sleep thinking of all the memories we had made together and where we stood in our future relationship. I knew I loved the Baron, but could it be that I also loved Buttons? I fell asleep with both dogs sleeping next to me and helping me relax with their sweet energy. I could feel their love for me and knew they loved me, too.

The morning came with a chill in the air and a frigid forecast that predicted snow by the end of the day. I would prepare to wear warmer clothes for my evening with Buttons. After a long walk with the dogs in Central Park, I came home to drop them off and head over for a massage. This was exactly what the doctor ordered.

I arrived back at the apartment to start getting ready for the evening. I took a hot bath and put some music on to feel relaxed. I opened a bottle of champagne and poured myself a glass. This was the beginning of a perfect celebration with Buttons. I was dressed and ready to receive him around 7 o'clock. My doorman called me and announced that Buttons was downstairs. "Please send him up."

All kinds of nervousness came over me, for the excitement of seeing him overwhelmed me. We hadn't seen each other for some time, and this was a special evening. I opened the door before he arrived to sing Happy Birthday when he walked up. He hugged me like he didn't want me ever to leave his arms. He had a very strong physical appearance, with muscular arms, a great smile, and a great body.

"What's up, gorgeous?" I could tell he was full of fun this evening.

"It's your birthday, handsome, and let's go celebrate you! I have a little something for you inside. Come on in, and we will have a glass of Champagne, and you can open my gift for you."

He walked in and grabbed a glass of Champagne. "Here's to you, Button, on your birthday." He reached over and gave me a kiss.

Love was in the air, or maybe a lot of lust.

"I've got you a little something. Open it now or when we come back."

He smiled at me and answered, "Let's open this later. I am so hungry that I wouldn't appreciate it now unless it was something to eat." He had a strange sense of humor.

"Let's go, and you can open it later." I took the flutes into the kitchen and grabbed my coat along with

my gloves. "I am ready to celebrate YOU."

We hailed a cab and had him drive us to this little romantic Italian restaurant in Midtown. My favorite restaurant with a very special guy. He kissed me, and I opened the door to get out after him. "Happy Birthday."

The clouds in the sky looked like they were ready to snow, and love surrounded the universe, which we were part of that night. We sat down and ate a quick dinner with only one thing in mind. We couldn't stop feeling each other under the table, and then we got the check so we could get out of there. Once we finished dinner and a bottle of wine, we decided to head back to my apartment. The sexual feelings between us were undeniably off the chart on every level.

Our lips touched, and we waited for the next passionate kiss from each other. We felt so alive at that moment. "Could this be love or pure lust?" Once upstairs in my apartment, clothes started coming off without missing a beat. Kissing and touching each other felt so sensuous that it felt like an out-of-body experience. We started to make love to each other until that moment of climax when we stopped and looked at one another.

A passionate feeling of "I LOVE YOU" surrendered from the heart. This was the beginning of something completely beyond comprehension. When hearts connect with the body and soul, a euphoric feeling of bliss is created from within, sending radiant feelings throughout the being. This experience was without words to describe it: "BREATHTAKING." This was so intoxicating for me. Our love transcended reality on all levels. It would transform into many dimensions throughout the heart. We couldn't get enough of each other, and feeling so much passion sent us both into a deep sleep in each other's arms. The morning arrived in my room, and it was snowing outside my window but hot inside my bed.

I rolled over to kiss him when he rolled over with a lot more on his mind. Lovemaking in the morning seemed to excite him. The amazing sexual experience with him sent me into an intense orbit, and I loved it. It was a place I could stay forever.

***

"Grandma, you have really done it now. You are at a crossroads with these two men. Where would you go from here?" Brian asked.

"You will have to wait and find out."

To Be Continued...

L. M. Lapham

About the Book

A love that comes along once in a lifetime is an enriching experience, expanding the human soul to unlimited boundaries. Love is a complicated flutter of emotional sensation that transcends time and distance. A love that touches the very cores of two hearts forever is a love so rare, so profound.

In a transformative journey, Katherine discovers a once-in-a-lifetime love to limitless horizons. Amidst the complexity of emotions, she's left pondering: can she hold feelings for two individuals at the same time? Is it possible to love them equally?

A fairy tale worth telling, choices worth making, and life-changing events that would shape the future of many lives involved in the experience. This story had passion, sex, money, privilege, and pain. How could a life-changing experience feel so right and go so wrong, or was it really wrong?

This is a love story—or should I say stories—about realizing the possibility of having two lovers and choosing which one would be Katherine's true love.

www.ingramcontent.com/pod-product-compliance
Lightning Source LLC
Chambersburg PA
CBHW040858010826
48978CB00013BA/1073